Books by Lawrence Block

The Bernie Rhodenbarr Mysteries

BURGLARS CAN'T BE CHOOSERS • THE BURGLAR IN THE
CLOSET • THE BURGLAR WHO LIKED TO QUOTE KIPLING •
THE BURGLAR WHO STUDIED SPINOZA • THE BURGLAR WHO
PAINTED LIKE MONDRIAN • THE BURGLAR WHO TRADED TED
WILLIAMS • THE BURGLAR WHO THOUGHT HE WAS BOGART
• THE BURGLAR IN THE LIBRARY • THE BURGLAR IN THE RYE •
THE BURGLAR ON THE PROWL

The Matthew Scudder Novels

THE SINS OF THE FATHERS • TIME TO MURDER AND CREATE • IN
THE MIDST OF DEATH • A STAB IN THE DARK • EIGHT MILLION
WAYS TO DIE • WHEN THE SACRED GINMILL CLOSES • OUT ON
THE CUTTING EDGE • A TICKET TO THE BONEYARD • A DANCE
AT THE SLAUGHTERHOUSE • A WALK AMONG THE TOMBSTONES
• THE DEVIL KNOWS YOU'RE DEAD • A LONG LINE OF DEAD
MEN • EVEN THE WICKED • EVERYBODY DIES • HOPE TO DIE •
ALL THE FLOWERS ARE DYING

Keller's Greatest Hits

HIT MAN • HIT LIST • HIT PARADE

The Adventures of Evan Tanner

THE THIEF WHO COULDN'T SLEEP • THE CANCELED CZECH •
TANNER'S TWELVE SWINGERS • THE SCORELESS THAI •
TANNER'S TIGER • TANNER'S VIRGIN • ME TANNER, YOU JANE
• TANNER ON ICE

SMALL TOWN

Collected Short Stories

ENOUGH ROPE

THE
THIEF
WHO
COULDN'T
SLEEP

THE FIRST
EVAN TANNER
NOVEL

LAWRENCE
BLOCK

HARPER

An Imprint of HarperCollinsPublishers

This book is a work of fiction. The characters, incidents, and dialogue are drawn from the author's imagination and are not to be construed as real. Any resemblance to actual events or persons, living or dead, is entirely coincidental.

HARPER

An Imprint of HarperCollins*Publishers*
195 Broadway
New York, NY 10007

Copyright © 1966 by Lawrence Block
Afterword copyright © 2007 by Lawrence Block
ISBN: 978-0-06-125806-0
ISBN-10: 0-06-125806-7

First Harper paperback printing: July 2007

HarperCollins® and Harper® are registered trademarks of HarperCollins Publishers.

Printed in the United States of America

Visit Harper paperbacks on the World Wide Web at
www.harpercollins.com

10 9 8 7 6 5 4 3

For Dave, Terri,
and Captain Bolshevik

THE
THIEF
WHO
COULDN'T
SLEEP

Chapter 1

The Turks have dreary jails. Or is that conjecture? The plural might be inaccurate, for all I truly knew, there might be but one jail in all of Turkey. Or there could be others, but they need not be dreary places at all. I sketched them mentally, a bevy of Turkish Delights bedecked with minarets, their floors and walls sparkling with embedded rubies, their dazzling halls patrolled by undraped Turkish maidens, and even the bars on the windows lovingly polished to a glowing sheen.

But, whatever the case, there was at least one dreary jail in Turkey. It was in Istanbul, it was dank and dirty and desolate, and I was in it. The floor of my cell could have been covered by a nine-by-twelve rug, but that would have hidden the decades of filth that had left their stamp upon the wooden floor. There was one small barred window, too small to let very much air in or out, too high to afford more than a glimpse of the sky. When the window turned dark, it was presumably night; when it grew blue again, I guessed that morning had come. But, of course, I could not be certain that the window even opened to the outside. For all I knew, some idiot Turk alternately lit and extinguished a lamp outside that window to provide me with this illusion.

A single twenty-five-watt bulb hung from the ceiling and kept my cell the same shade of gray day and night. I'd been provided with a sagging army cot and a folding cardtable chair. There was a chamber pot in one corner of my chamber. The cell door was a simple affair of vertical bars, through which I could see a bank of empty cells opposite. I never saw another prisoner, never heard a human sound except for the Turkish guard who seemed to be assigned to me. He came morning, noon, and night with food. Breakfast was always a slab of cold black toast and a cup of thick black coffee. Lunch and dinner were always the same—a tin plate piled with a suspicious pilaff, mostly rice with occasional bits of lamb and shreds of vegetable matter of indeterminate origin. Incredibly enough, the pilaff was delicious. I lived in constant fear that misguided humanitarian impulses might lead my captors to vary my monotonous diet, substituting something inedible for the blessed pilaff. But twice a day my guard brought pilaff, and twice a day I wolfed it down.

It was the boredom that was stifling. I had been arrested on a Tuesday. I'd flown to Istanbul from Athens, arriving around ten in the morning, and I knew something had gone wrong when the customs officer took far too much time pawing through my suitcase. When he sighed at last and closed the bag, I said, "Are you quite through?"

"Yes. You are Evan Tanner?"

"Yes."

"Evan Michael Tanner?"

"Yes."

"American?"

"Yes."

"You flew from New York to London, from London to Athens, and from Athens to Istanbul?"

"Yes."

"You have business in Istanbul?"

"Yes."

He smiled. "You are under arrest," he said.

"Why?"

"I am sorry," he said, "but I am not at liberty to say."

My crime seemed destined to remain a secret forever. Three uniformed Turks drove me to jail in a jeep. A clerk took my watch, my belt, my passport, my suitcase, my necktie, my shoelaces, my pocket comb and my wallet. He wanted my ring, but it wouldn't leave my finger, so he let me keep it. My uniformed bodyguard led me down a flight of stairs, through a catacombic maze of corridors, and ushered me into a cell.

There was nothing much to do in that cell. I don't sleep, have not slept in sixteen years—more of that later—so I had the special joy of being bored, not sixteen hours a day, like the normal prisoner, but a full twenty-four. I ached for something to read, anything at all. Wednesday night I asked my guard if he could bring me some books or magazines.

"I don't speak English," he said in Turkish.

I *do* speak Turkish, but I thought it might be worthwhile to keep this a secret. "Just a book or a magazine," I said in English. "Even an old newspaper."

In Turkish he said, "Your mother loves to perform fellatio upon syphilitic dogs."

I took the proffered plate of pilaff. "Your fly is open," I said in English.

He looked down immediately. His fly was not open, and his eyes focused reproachfully on me. "I don't speak English," he said again in Turkish. "Your mother spreads herself for camels."

Dogs, camels. He went away, and I ate the pilaff and wondered what had led them to arrest me, and precisely why they were holding me, and if they would ever let me go. My guard pretended he could not speak English, and I feigned ignorance of Turkish. The high window turned alternately blue and black, the guard brought toast and pilaff and pilaff, toast and pilaff and pilaff, toast and pilaff and pilaff. The chamber pot began to approach capacity, and I amused myself by calculating just when it would overflow and by trying to imagine how I might bring this to the attention of a guard who refused to admit to a knowledge of English. Would either of us lose face if we talked in French?

The pattern changed, finally, on my ninth day in jail, a Wednesday. I thought it was Tuesday—I'd lost a day somewhere—but it turned out that I was wrong. I had my usual breakfast, paid my usual tribute to my chamber pot, and performed a brief regimen of setting-up exercises. An hour or so after breakfast I heard footsteps in the hallway. My guard unlocked my door, and two uniformed men came into my cell. One was very tall, very thin, very much the officer. The other was shorter, fatter, sweaty, and moustached, and possessed an abundance of gold teeth.

Both carried clipboards and wore sidearms. The tall one studied his clipboard for a moment, then looked at me. "You are Evan Tanner," he said.

"Yes."

He smiled. "I believe we will be able to release you very shortly, Mr. Tanner," he said. "I regret the need to have dealt so unpleasantly with you, but I'm sure you can understand."

"No, I can't, frankly."

He studied me. "Why, there were so many points to be checked, and naturally it was necessary to keep you in a safe place while these checks were made. And then you acted in such a strange manner, you know. You never questioned your confinement, you never banged furiously on the bars of your cell, you never slept—"

"I don't sleep."

"But we did not know that then, don't you see?" He smiled again. "You did not demand to see the American ambassador. Every American invariably demands to see the ambassador. If an American is overcharged in a restaurant, he wants to bring the matter at once to his ambassador's attention. But you seemed to accept everything—"

I said, "When rape is inevitable, lie back and enjoy it."

"What? Oh, I see. But that is a sophisticated reaction, you understand, and it called for explanation. We contacted Washington and learned quite a great deal about you. Not everything, I am quite certain, but a great deal." He looked around the cell. "Perhaps you've tired of your surroundings. Let us find more comfortable quarters. I must ask you several questions, and then you will be free to go."

We left the cell. The short man with the gold teeth led the way, my interrogator and I followed side by side, and my guard trailed along a few paces behind. Walking was awkward. I'd evidently lost a little weight, and my beltless pants had to be held up manually. My shoes, lacking laces, kept slipping off my feet.

In an airy cleaner room a floor above, the taller man sat beneath a flattering portrait of Ataturk and smiled benevolently at me. He asked if I knew why they had arrested me so promptly. I said that I did not.

"Would you care to know?"

"Of course."

"You are a member"—he consulted the clipboard—"of a fascinating array of organizations, Mr. Tanner. We did not know just how many causes had caught your interest, but when your name appeared on the incoming passenger list it did line up with our membership rosters for two rather interesting organizations. You belong, it would seem, to the Pan-Hellenic Friendship Society. True?"

"Yes."

"And to the League for the Restoration of Cilician Armenia?"

"Yes."

He stroked his chin. "Neither of these two organizations is particularly friendly to Turkish interests, Mr. Tanner. Each is composed of a scattering of—how would you say it? Fanatics? Yes, fanatics. The Pan-Hellenic Friendship Society has been extremely vocal lately. We suspect they're peripherally involved in some acts of minor terrorism over Cyprus. The Armenian fanatics have been dormant since the close of the war. Most people would probably be surprised to know that they even exist, and we've had no trouble from them for a very long time. But suddenly you appear in Istanbul and are recognized as a member of not one but both of these organizations." He paused significantly. "It might interest you to know that our records indicate you are the only man on earth to hold membership in both organizations."

"Is that so?"

"Yes."

"That's very interesting," I said.

He offered me a cigarette. I declined. He took one

himself and lit it. The smell of Turkish tobacco was overpowering.

"Would you care to explain these memberships, Mr. Tanner?"

I thought this over. "I'm a joiner," I said finally.

"Yes, I'm sure you are."

"I'm a member of . . . many groups."

"Indeed." He referred to the clipboard once more. "Our list may not be complete, but you may fill in any significant omissions. You belong to the two groups I mentioned. You also belong to the Irish Republican Brotherhood and the Clann-na-Gaille. You are a member of the Flat Earth Society of England, the Macedonian Friendship League, the Industrial Workers of the World, the Libertarian League, the Society for a Free Croatia, the Confederación Nacional del Trabajadores de España, the Committee Allied Against Fluoridation, the Serbian Brotherhood, the Nazdóya Fedèróvka, and the Lithuanian Army-in-Exile." He looked up and sighed. "This list goes on and on. Need I read more?"

"I'm impressed with your research."

"A simple call to Washington, Mr. Tanner. They have a lengthy file on you, did you know that?"

"Yes."

"Why on earth do you belong to all these groups? According to Washington, you don't seem to *do* anything. You attend an occasional meeting, you receive an extraordinary quantity of pamphlets, you associate with subversives of every conceivable persuasion, but you don't do much of anything. Can you explain yourself?"

"Lost causes interest me."

"Pardon?"

It seemed pointless to explain it to him, as pointless as the many sessions I'd had with FBI agents over the years. The charm of an organization devoted to a singularly hopeless cause is evidently lost on the average person and certainly on the average bureaucrat or policeman. One either appreciates the beauty of a band of three hundred men scattered across the face of the earth with nothing more on their mind, say, than the utterly unattainable dream of separating Wales from the United Kingdom—one either finds this heartrendingly marvelous or dismisses the little band as a batch of nuts and cranks.

But, however futile my explanation, I knew that a slew of words of any sort would be better in this Turk's eyes than my silence. I talked, and he listened and stared at me, and when I finished he sat silent for a moment and then shook his head.

"You astound me," he said.

There seemed no need for a reply.

"It seemed quite obvious to us that you were an *agent provocateur*. We contacted your American Central Intelligence Agency, and they denied any knowledge of you, which made us all the more certain you were one of their agents. We're still not certain that you're not. But you don't fit any of the standard molds. You don't make any sense."

"That's true," I said.

"You don't sleep. You're thirty-four years old and lost the power to sleep when you were eighteen. Is that correct?"

"Yes."

"In the war?"

"Korea."

"Turkey sent troops to Korea," he said.

This was indisputably true, but it seemed a conversational dead end. This time I decided to wait him out. He put out his cigarette and shook his head sadly at me.

"You were shot through the head? Is that what happened?"

"More or less. A piece of shrapnel. Nothing seemed damaged—it was just a fleck of shrapnel, actually—so they patched me up and gave me my gun and sent me back into battle. Then I just wasn't sleeping, not at all. I didn't know why. They thought it was mental—something like that. The trauma of being wounded. It was nothing like that because the wound hadn't shaken me up much at all. I never knew I was hit at the time, not until someone noticed I was bleeding a little from the forehead, so there wasn't any trauma involved. Then they—"

"What is trauma?"

"Shock."

"I see. Continue."

"Well, they kept knocking me out with shots, and I would stay out until the shot wore off and then wake up again. They couldn't even induce normal sleep. They decided finally that the sleep center of my brain was destroyed. They're not sure just what the sleep center is or just how it works, but evidently I don't have one any more. So I don't sleep."

"Not at all?"

"Not at all."

"Don't you become tired?"

"Of course. I rest when I'm tired. Or switch from a mental activity to a physical one, or vice versa."

"But you can just go on and on without sleep?"

"Yes."

"That is incredible."

It isn't, of course. Science still doesn't know what makes men sleep, or how, or why. Men will die without it. If you keep a man forcibly awake, he will die sooner than if you starve him. And yet, no one knows what sleep does for the body or how it comes on a person.

"You are in good health, Mr. Tanner?"

"Yes."

"Is it not a strain on your heart, this endless wakefulness?"

"It doesn't seem to be."

"And you'll live as long as anyone else?"

"Not quite as long, according to the doctors. Their statistics indicate that I'll live three-fourths of my natural life span, barring accidents, of course. But I don't trust their figures. The condition just doesn't occur often enough to afford any conclusions."

"But they say you won't live as long."

"Yes. Though my insomnia probably won't cut off as many years from my life as would smoking, for example."

He frowned. He'd just lit a fresh cigarette and didn't enjoy being reminded of its ill effects. So he changed the subject.

"How do you live?" he asked.

"From day to day."

"You misunderstand me. How do you earn your living?"

"I receive a disability pension from the Army. For my loss of sleep."

"They pay you one hundred twelve dollars per month. Is that correct?"

It was. I've no idea how the Defense Department had arrived at that sum. I'm certain there's no precedent.

"You do not live on one hundred twelve dollars per month. What else do you do? You are not employed, are you?"

"Self-employed."

"How?"

"I write doctoral dissertations and master's theses."

"I do not understand."

"I write theses and term papers for students. They turn them in as their own work. Occasionally I take examinations for them as well—at Columbia or New York University."

"Is this allowed?"

"No."

"I see. You help them cheat?"

"I help them compensate for their personal inadequacies."

"There is a name for this profession? It is a recognized profession?"

The hell with him, I decided. The hell with him and his questions and his rotten jail. "I'm called a stentaphator," I explained. He had me spell it and he wrote it down very carefully. "Stentaphators are subsidiary scholars concerned with suasion and ambidexterity."

He didn't know *trauma;* I was fairly sure *suasion* and *ambidexterity* would ring no bells, and I guessed he wouldn't ask for definitions. His English was excellent, his accent only slight. The only weapon in my arsenal was double-talk.

He lit still another cigarette—the man was going to smoke himself sick—and narrowed his eyes at me. "Why are you in Turkey, Mr. Tanner?"

"I'm a tourist."

"Don't be absurd. You've never left the United States since Korea, according to Washington. You applied for a passport less than three months ago. You came at once to Istanbul. Why?"

I hesitated.

"For whom are you spying, Mr. Tanner? The CIA? One of your little organizations? Tell me."

"I'm not spying at all."

"Then why are you here?"

I hesitated. Then I said, "There is a man in Antakya who makes counterfeit gold coins. He's noted for his counterfeit Armenian pieces, but he does other work as well. Marvelous work. According to Turkish law, he's able to do this with impunity. He never counterfeits Turkish coins, so it's all perfectly legal."

"Continue."

"I plan to see him, buy an assortment of coins, smuggle them back into the United States, and sell them as genuine."

"It is a violation of Turkish law to remove antiquities from the country."

"These are not antiquities. The man makes them himself. I intended to have him give me an affidavit testifying that the coins were forgeries. It's a violation of U.S. law to bring gold into the country in any form, and it's a case of fraud to sell a counterfeit coin as genuine, but I was prepared to take that chance." I smiled. "I had no intention, though, of violating Turkish law. You may believe me."

The man looked at me for a long time. Finally he said, "That is an extraordinary explanation."

"It happens to be true."

"You sat for nine days in jail with an explanation in your pocket that would have gotten you released at once. That argues for its truth, does it not? Otherwise you might have told your cover story right away, accompanied it with a bribe, and attempted to get out of our hands the very first day; before we began to learn so many interesting things about you. A counterfeiter in Antakya. Armenian gold coins, for the love of God. When did Armenians make gold coins?"

"In the Middle Ages."

"One moment, please." He used a phone on his desk and called someone. I looked up at Ataturk's portrait and listened to his conversation. He was asking some bureaucrat somewhere if there was in fact a counterfeiter in Antakya and what sort of things the man produced. He was not overly surprised to find out that my story checked out.

To me he said, "If you are lying, you have built your lie on true foundations. I find it frankly inconceivable that you would travel to Istanbul for such a purpose. There is a profit in it?"

"I could buy a thousand dollars worth of rare forgeries and sell them for thirty thousand dollars by passing them as genuine."

"Is that true?"

"Yes."

He was silent for a moment. "I still do not believe you," he said at length. "You are a spy or a saboteur of one sort or another. I am convinced of it. But it makes no matter. Whatever you are, whatever your intentions, you must leave Turkey. You are unwelcome in our country, and there are men in your own country who are very much interested in speaking with you.

"Mustafa will see that you get a bath and a chance to change your clothes. At three-fifteen this afternoon you will board a Pan American flight for Shannon Airport. Mustafa will be with you. You will have two hours between planes and you will then board another

Pan American flight for Washington, where Mustafa will turn you over to agents of your own government." Mustafa, who was to do all this, was the grubby little man who had brought my pilaff twice a day and my toast each morning. If he was important enough to accompany me to Washington, then he was a rather high-level type to use as a prison guard, which meant that I was probably thought to be the greatest threat on earth to the peace and security of the Republic of Turkey.

"We will not see you again," he went on. "I do not doubt that the United States Government will revoke your passport. Unless you are, in fact, their agent, which is still quite possible. I am beyond caring. Nothing you tell me makes any sense, and everything is probably a lie. I believe nothing that anyone tells me in this day and age."

"It's the safest course," I assured him.

"In any case, you will never return to Turkey. You are *persona non grata* here. You will leave, taking with you all of the personal belongings you brought in with you. You will leave and you will not return for any reason."

"That suits me."

"I hoped it would." He stood up, dismissing me, and Mustafa led me toward the door.

"A moment—"

I turned.

"Tell me one thing," he said. "Precisely what is the Flat Earth Society of England?"

"It's worldwide, really. Not limited to England, although it was organized there and has most of its members there."

"But what is it?"

"A group of people who believe the earth is flat,

rather than round. The society is devoted to propagating this belief and winning converts to this way of thinking."

He stared at me. I stared back.

"Flat," he said. "Are these people crazy?"

"No more than you or I."

I left him with that to contemplate. Mustafa led me to a rudimentary bathroom and stood outside while I washed an impressive amount of filth from my body. When I got out of the shower he handed me my suitcase. I put on clean clothes and closed my suitcase. I tied my dirty clothing into a fetid bundle—shoes and socks and all—and passed the reeking mess to Mustafa. He was not an overly clean man himself, but he took a step backward at once.

"In the name of peace and friendship and the International Brotherhood of Stentaphators, I present this clothing as a gift and tribute unto the great Republic of Turkey."

"I don't speak English," Mustafa lied.

"What the hell does that mean?" I demanded. "Oh, the devil with you."

We stopped at the clerk's desk. I was given back my belt, my necktie, my shoelaces, my pocket comb, my wallet, and my watch. Mustafa took my passport and tucked it away in a pocket. I asked him for it, and he grinned and told me he didn't speak English.

We left the building. The sun was absolutely blinding. My eyes were unequal to it. I wondered if Mustafa would consider dropping his pose of not speaking English. We would have a long flight together. Would he want to pass the whole trip in stony silence?

I decided that I could probably get him to talk, but

that it might be better if I didn't. A silent Mustafa could well be more bearable than a talkative one, especially since I would be able to pick up some paperbacks to read on the plane. And I did seem to have an advantage. He spoke English and didn't know I knew it. I spoke Turkish, and he didn't know that, either. Why give up that sort of edge?

We walked along toward a 1953 Chevrolet, its fenders crippled, its body riddled with rust. We sat in back, and Mustafa told the driver to take us to the airport. He leaned forward, and I heard him tell the driver that I was a very deceptive spy from the United States of America and that I was emphatically not to be trusted.

They all see too many James Bond movies. They expect spies everywhere and overlook the profit motive entirely. A spy? It was the last thing on earth I would ever become. I had no intentions of spying for or against Turkey or anyone else.

I had come, quite simply, so that I could steal approximately three million dollars in gold.

Chapter 2

It had begun some months before in Manhattan at the junction of three streams—a job, a girl, and a most noble lost cause. The job involved preparation of a thesis that would win Brian Cudahy a master's degree in history from Columbia University. The girl was Kitty Bazerian, who rolls her belly in Chelsea nightclubs as Alexandra the Great. The noble lost cause, one of the noblest, one of the most utterly lost, was the League for the Restoration of Cilician Armenia.

I first saw Brian Cudahy on a Saturday morning. My mail had just arrived, and I was sitting in my living room sorting it. I receive a tremendous amount of mail. I'm on hundreds of mailing lists and I subscribe to a great many periodicals, and my mail carrier detests me. I live on 107th Street a few doors west of Broadway. My neighbors are transients and addicts and students and Orientals and actors and harlots, six classes of people who get little in the way of mail. Bills from Con Ed and the telephone company, slingers from the supermarkets, quarterly messages from their congressman, little else. I, on the other hand, burden my mailman with a sack of paper garbage every day.

My bell rang. I pressed a buzzer to admit my caller into the building. He climbed four flights of stairs and hesitated in the hallway. I waited, and he knocked, and I opened the door.

"Tanner?"

"Yes."

"I'm Brian Cudahy. I called you last night—"

"Oh, yes," I said. "Come in." He seated himself in the rocking chair. "Coffee?"

"If it's no trouble."

I made instant coffee in the kitchen and brought back two cups. He was looking all over the apartment. I suppose it's a little unusual. People have said that it looks more like a library than an apartment. There are four rooms besides the kitchen and the bath, and in each room the walls are done in floor-to-ceiling bookcases, almost all of which are full. Beyond that, there's rather little in the way of furniture. I've a large bed in one room, a very large writing desk in another, a few chairs scattered here and there, and a small dresser in still another room, and that's about all. I don't find the place unusual at all, myself. When one is a compulsive reader and researcher and when one has a full twenty-four hours a day at his disposal, not having to allot eight for sleep and eight for work, one certainly ought to have plenty of books on hand.

"Is the coffee all right?"

"Oh!" He looked up, startled. "Yes, of course. I . . . uh . . . I'm going to need your help. Mr. Tanner."

He was about twenty-four, I guessed. Clean-cut, bright-faced, short-haired, with an air of incipient success about him. He looked like a student but not at all like a scholar. An increasing number of such persons pursue graduate degrees these days. Industry considers a bachelor's degree indispensable and, by a curious extension, regards master's degrees and doctorates as a way of separating the men from the boys. I don't understand this. Why should a Ph.D. awarded for an extended essay on color symbolism in the poetry of Pushkin have anything to do with a man's competence to develop a sales promotion campaign for a manufacturer of ladies' underwear?

"My thesis is due the middle of next month," Cudahy was saying. "I can't seem to get anywhere on it. And I heard that you . . . you were recommended as—"

"As one who writes theses?"

He nodded.

"What's your field?" I asked.

"History."

"You've a topic already assigned, of course."

"Yes."

"What is it?"

He swallowed. "Sort of offbeat, I'm afraid."

"Good."

"Excuse me?"

"Offbeat topics are the best. What's yours?"

"The Turkish persecutions of Armenians during the late nineteenth century and immediately before and after the First World War." He grinned. "Don't ask me how I got saddled with that one. I can't figure it out, myself. Do you know anything about the subject, Mr. Tanner?"

"Yes."

"You do?" He was incredulous. "Honestly?"

"I know a great deal about it," I said.

"Then can you . . . uh . . . write the thesis?"

"Probably. Have you done anything on it to date?"

"I have notes here—"

"Notes that you've shown an instructor or just your own work?"

"No one's seen anything yet. I've had some oral conferences with my instructor but nothing very important."

I waved his briefcase aside. "Then I'd rather not see your notes," I told him. "I find it easier to start fresh if you don't mind."

"You'll do it?"

"For seven hundred fifty dollars."

His face clouded. "That seems high. I don't—"

"A master's degree is worth an extra fifteen hundred to industry the first year. That's minimal. I'm charging you half your first year's differential. If you try to haggle, the price goes up, not down."

"It's a deal."

"This is for Columbia, you said?"

"Yes."

"And your grades have been—"

"B average."

"All right. About a hundred-page thesis? And you want it the middle of next month?"

"Yes."

"You'll have it. Call me in three weeks, and I'll let you know how it's coming along."

"Three weeks."

"Don't call before then. And I'll want half the money now, if it's all the same to you."

"I don't have it on me. Can I bring it this afternoon?"

"You do that," I said.

He was back at two that afternoon with $375 in cash. He was just a little reluctant to part with it—I don't think because he would miss the money so much but because this made the deal firm, committed him to a plan that he knew very well was morally reprehensible.

He was purchasing his master's degree. It would be a big status thing for him, that master's, and he'd have gotten it unfairly, and it would always bother him a little, and he knew as much already. But he handed me the money, and I took it, and we both sealed our pact with the devil.

"I suppose you've done lots of theses," he said.

"Quite a number."

"Many in history?"

"Yes. And a good number in English, and a few in sociology and economics. And some other things."

"What did you do your own on?"

"My own?"

"Your master's and doctorate."

"I don't even have a bachelor's," I told him truthfully. "I joined the Army the day I left high school. Korea. I never did go to college."

He found this extraordinary. He talked about how easy it would be for me to go through college and walk off with highest honors. "It would be a snap for you. Why, you could write your thesis with no sweat. The exams, the whole routine. It would be nothing for you."

"Exactly," I said.

Cudahy's thesis was a very simple matter. I already knew quite a good deal about the Terrible Turk and the Starving Armenians. My library contained all the basic texts on the subject and more than a few lesser-known works, including several in Armenian. I speak Armenian, but reading it is a chore. The alphabet is unfamiliar and the construction tedious. I also had an almost complete file of the publications in English of the League for the Restoration of Cilician Armenia. Biased though they were, the League's pamphlets could not fail to impress in a bibliography.

It was pleasant work. Research is a joy, especially when one is not burdened with an excessive reverence for the truth. By inventing an occasional source and injecting an occasional spurious footnote, one softens the harsh curves in the royal road of scholarship. I studied, I ate, I worked out at the 110th Street Gym, I read, I kept up my correspondence, and I developed Cudahy's thesis with little difficulty.

I narrowed his topic somewhat, focusing on the Armenian Nationalist movements that had in large part provoked the Turkish massacres. Hunchak and Daschnak, organized in 1885 and 1890 respectively, had worked to develop a national consciousness and pressed for liberation from the Ottoman Empire. The minor Kurdish massacre of 1894 led to an absorbing parade of Big Power manipulations and was followed a year later by Abdu-l-Hamid's mammoth slaughter of eighty thousand Armenians.

But it was during World War I, when Turkey fought on the Axis side and feared her Armenian subjects as a potential fifth column, that the Armenian massacres reached their height and the phrase "Starving Armenians" found its way into our language. In mid-1915 the Turks went berserk. In one community after another the Armenian population was uprooted, men and women and children were massacred indiscriminately, and those who were not put to the sword either fled the country or quietly starved.

After the war the Soviets took Armenia proper, establishing an Armenian Soviet Socialist Republic. The areas that remained Turkish had largely lost their Armenian population. The last large concentration of Armenians to suffer en masse were those in the city of Smyrna, now Izmir. The Greeks seized the town in the Greco-Turkish War that followed close upon the signing of the armistice. When Ataturk recaptured Smyrna, the city was burned, and the Greeks and Armenians were systematically destroyed. An earthquake further reduced the city in 1928, but by that time there were few Armenians left in it.

Smyrna, then, was an afterthought, a sort of footnote to the whole business. My main focus was on the Nationalist movements, their organization, their development, their aims, and their ultimate effects. I expected to finish the thesis well ahead of schedule and I expected to go no further with the study of the destruction of Smyrna. But I had not then met Kitty or her grandmother.

Kitty and I met at a wedding in the Village. My friend Owen Morgan was being married to a Jewish girl from White Plains. Owen is a Welsh poet with no discernible talent who had discovered that one could make a fair living by drinking an impressive amount, spouting occasional poetry, seducing every comely female within reach, and generally behaving like the shade of Dylan Thomas. He startled me by asking me to be his best man, an office I had never before performed. So I stood up for him in a drab loft on Sullivan Street at the ceremony performed by a priest friendly to the Catholic Workers. Neither of them was Catholic, but Owen had lived at the CW settlement on Christie Street for a few months before he discovered the potential of the Dylan Thomas bit. (I'm a member of the Catholic Workers myself, although I don't give them as much of my time as I probably should. They're a wonderful organization.) I stood up for Owen and passed him the ring at the appropriate time, and afterward Kitty Bazerian danced at his wedding.

She was small and slender and dark, with fine black hair and huge brown eyes. She stood demurely, garbed in a wisp of diaphanous fluff, and someone said, "Now Kitty Bazerian will dance for us," and the house band from the New Life Restaurant began to play, and her body sang in the center of the improvised stage, music in motion, silk, velvet, perfection, adding a wholly new dimension to sensuality.

Afterward I found her at the bar, dressed now in skirt and sweater and black tights, which was about right for Owen's wedding.

"Alexandra the Great," I said.

"Who told you? They promised not to say."

"I recognized you myself."

"Honestly?"

"I've watched you dance at the New Life. And at the Port Said before that."

"And you recognized me right away?"

"Of course. I never knew that Alexandra the Great was an Armenian."

"A starving Armenian right about now. Aren't they having anything to eat?"

"It would spoil Owen's image."

"I suppose we have to respect his image. But I already had too much to drink and I'm starving."

"May it never be said that Evan Tanner let an Armenian starve. Why don't we get out of here?"

We did. I suggested the Sayat Nova at Bleecker and Charles. She asked me why I was so very hipped on Armenians. I told her I was writing a thesis on Armenia.

"You're a student?"

"No, I'm just writing a thesis."

"I don't . . . wait a minute, you're Evan *Tanner!* Sure, Owen told me about you. He says you're crazier than he is."

"He may be right."

"And you're writing about Armenians now? You ought to meet my grandmother. She could tell you all about how we lost the family fortunes. She makes a good story out of it. According to her, we were the richest Armenians in Turkey. Gold coins, she says; more gold coins than you could count. And now the Turks have it all." She laughed. "Isn't that always the way? Owen insists he's a direct descendant of Owen Glendower and the rightful King of all of Wales. The Sayat Nova sounds fine, Evan. But I warn you, I'm going to be expensive. I'll eat everything they've got."

"I don't remember what we had or how it tasted. There was a good red wine with the meal, but we got drunker on each other than on anything else. It does not happen often for me, the special magic, the perfect harmony. It happened this time.

She talked some about her dancing. I was delighted to discover that she had no higher ambitions. She did not want to become a ballerina, or get a guest shot on the Sullivan show, or found a new school of modern dance. She just wanted to go on dancing at the New Life for as long as they wanted her.

I, on the other hand, have many ambitions and I told her of them. "Someday," I confided, "we'll restore the House of Stuart to the English throne. The Jacobite movement has never entirely died out, you know. There are men in the Scottish Highlands who would rise at any moment to throw out those Hanoverian interlopers."

"You're putting me on—"

"Oh, no," I said, wagging a finger at her. "The last reigning Stuart was Anne. She died in 1714 and they brought over a Hanoverian, a German. George I. And ever since that day the Germans have sat upon the English throne. If you think about it, it's an outrage."

"But the House of Stuart—"

"There have been attempts," I said. "Bonnie Prince Charlie in 1745. All of Scotland rose to support him, but the French didn't do all they were supposed to do, and nothing came of it. The English won the Battle of Culloden Moor and thought that was the end of it." I paused significantly. "But they were wrong."

"They were?"

"The House of Stuart has not died out, Kitty. There has always been a Stuart Pretender to the English throne, although some of them have worked harder at it than others. The current Pretender is Rupert. Someday he'll reign as Rupert I, after Betty Saxe-Coburg and her German court have been routed."

"Betty Saxe-Coburg . . . oh, Elizabeth, of course. And who is Rupert?"

"He's a Bavarian crown prince."

She looked at me for a long moment and then began to laugh. "Oh, that's beautiful! That's priceless, Evan. I love it!"

"Do you?"

"Replacing the . . . the German usurpers with . . . oh, it's *great* . . . with the crown prince of *Bavaria*—"

"The true English claimant."

"I love it. Oh, sign me up, Evan. It's better than a Barbara Stanwyck movie. Oh, it's grand. I love it!"

And outside, a breeze playing with her marvelous black hair, she said, "I live with my mother and my grandmother, so that's out. Do you have a place we can go to?"

"Yes."

"But Owen said something about you not sleeping. I mean—"

"I don't, but I have a bed."

"How sweet of you," she said, taking my arm, "to have a bed."

Chapter 3

It was about a week after that when I finally did meet Kitty's grandmother. Kitty had told me several times that I would enjoy the old woman's story, and she became especially enthusiastic when I showed her my membership card in the League for the Restoration of Cilician Armenia. She had never heard of the group—rather few people have, actually—but she was certain her grandmother would be delighted.

"She has some pretty grim memories," Kitty said. "She was the only one of the family to get away. The Turks killed everybody else. I have a feeling she got raped in the bargain, but she never said anything about it exactly, and it's not the kind of subject you discuss with your grandmother. If you're really interested in all this Armenian jazz, you'll enjoy her. And she's getting older, you know, and I think she may be getting a little flaky, so not many people listen to her very much any more."

"I'd love to meet her."

"Would you? She'll be all excited. She's like a kid sometimes."

Kitty lived in Brooklyn, just across the bridge, in a neighborhood that was largely Syrian and Lebanese with a scattering of Armenians. We walked from the subway. It was early afternoon. Her mother was out waiting on tables in a neighborhood diner. Her grandmother sat in front of the television set watching one of those afternoon game shows where everyone laughs and smiles all the time.

Kitty said, "Grandma, this is—"

"Wait," Grandma said. "See that lady, she just won a Pontiac convertible, can you imagine? Now she has to decide to keep it or trade it for what's behind the curtain. See, she don't know what's behind the curtain. She has to decide without looking. See!"

The woman traded. The curtain opened, and Grandma sucked in her breath, then exploded with strident laughter. Behind the curtain was a set of Teflon-coated aluminum frying pans.

"For this she trades the Pontiac convertible," Grandma said. "With four-speed transmission and power seats, can you believe it?" The woman who had made this mistake was crying bravely, and the emcee was smiling and saying something about it all being part of the game. "Ha!" said Grandma, and pressed a remote-control button to extinguish the program. "Now," she said, whirling around to face us. "Who is this? You're married, Katin?"

"No," Kitty-Katin said. "Grandma, this is Evan Tanner. He wanted to see you."

"To see me?"

She was a gnomish little woman, her still-black hair parted absurdly in the middle, a strange light dancing merrily in her brown eyes. She was smoking a Helmar cigarette and had a tall glass of a dangerous orange liquid beside her. This was her life—a chair in front of a television set in her daughter's house. It was extraordinary, her eyes said, that a young man would come to see her.

"He's a writer," Kitty explained. "He is very inter-

ested in the story of how you left Turkey. Of the riches
and the massacres and . . . uh . . . all of that."

"His name?"

"Evan Tanner."

"Tanner? He is Armenian?"

In Armenian I said, "I am not Armenian myself,
Mrs. Bazerian, but I have long been a great friend of
the Armenian people and their supporter in their heroic
fight for freedom."

Her eyes caught fire. "He speaks Armenian!" she
cried. "Katin, he speaks Armenian!"

"I knew she would love you," Kitty told me.

"Katin, make coffee. Mr. Tanner and I must talk.
When did you learn to speak Armenian, Mr. Tanner?
My own Katin cannot speak it. Her own mother can
speak it only poorly. Katin, make coffee the right way,
not this powder with water spilled in it. Mr. Tanner,
do you like coffee the Armenian way? If you cannot
stand the spoon upright in the cup, then the coffee is
too weak. We have a saying, you know, that coffee
must be 'hot as hell, black as sin, and sweet as love.'
But why am I speaking English with you? English I
can hear on the television set. Katin, do not stand there
foolishly. Make the coffee. Sit down, Mr. Tanner. Now,
what shall I tell you? Eh?"

I stayed for hours. She spoke a Turkish strain of Armenian, and I had learned the language as it was spoken in the area that was now the Armenian S.S.R. So
she was a bit hard to understand at first, but I caught the
flavor of the dialect before long and followed her with
little difficulty. She kept sending Kitty to fetch more
coffee and once she chased her around the block to a
bakery for baklava. She apologized for the baklava; it
was Syrian, she said, and not as light and subtle as Ar-

menian baklava. But that could not be helped, for there was no longer an Armenian baker in the neighborhood. The little rolled honey cakes were delicious, nevertheless, and Kitty made excellent coffee.

And the old woman's story was a classic. It had happened in 1922, she told me. She had been but a girl then, a girl just old enough to seek a husband. "And there were many who wanted me, Mr. Tanner. I was a pretty one then. And my father the richest man in Balikesir . . ."

Balikesir, a town about a hundred miles north of Smyrna, was the capital of Balikesir Province. She had lived there with her mother and her father and her father's father and two brothers and a sister and assorted aunts and uncles and cousins. Her father's house was one of the finest in Balikesir, and her father was the head of the town's Armenian community. A fine house it was, too, not far from the railroad station, built high upon a hill with a view for miles in all directions. A huge house, with high columns around the doorway and a sloping cement walk down to the street below. Of the five hundred Armenian families in Balikesir, none had a finer house.

"The Greeks were at war with the Turks," she told me. "Of course, we were on the side of the Greeks, and my father had raised funds for the Greeks and knew many of their leaders. There were thousands of Greeks in Balikesir, and they were good friends with the Armenians. Our churches were different, but we were all Christians, not heathens like the Turks. At first my father thought the Greeks would win. The British were going to help us, you see. But, then, no help came from the British, and my father learned that the Turks would win after all."

It was then that the gold began to come to the house in Balikesir. Every day men brought sacks of gold, she said. Some brought little leather purses, some brought suitcases, some had gold coins sewn into their garments. Each man brought the gold to her father, who counted it carefully and wrote out a receipt for it. Then the man left, and the gold was put in the basement.

"But we could not leave it there, you see. The bandits were already at the gates of Smyrna, and time was short. And my father had in his hands all the gold of all the Armenians of Smyrna."

"Of Balikesir, you mean?"

She laughed. "Of Balikesir? Oh, no. Why, there were only five hundred families of our people in Balikesir. No, they brought all the Armenian gold of Smyrna as well because they knew that Smyrna would fall first and they knew, too, that my father was a man who could be trusted. Just a few sacks would have held all the gold of Balikesir, but the riches of Smyrna—that was another matter."

Her father and his brothers had worked industriously. She recalled it all very well, she told me. One afternoon a man had come with news that Smyrna had fallen, and that very night the whole family had worked. There was a huge front porch on their house, wooden on the top, with concrete sides and front. That night her father and her uncle Poul broke through the concrete on the left side. Then the whole family carried the gold coins from the basement and hid them away beneath the porch.

They made many trips, she told me. They carried big sacks and little sacks, and once she had dropped a cloth purse, and the shiny coins had scattered all over the basement floor, and she had to scurry around picking them up and putting them back into the purse. Almost all the coins were the same, she said—a bit smaller than an American quarter, with a woman's head on one side and a man on horseback on the other, and the man, she remembered, was sticking something with a spear.

British sovereigns, of course. The head of Victoria (Vicki Hanover, *that* usurper) and the reverse was St. George slaying the dragon. That had been the most common gold coin in the Middle East, I knew; the most trusted gold piece, the coin one would choose to hoard as family or communal wealth.

At last all the coins were in place, Kitty's grandmother explained, and they filled the space beneath the porch to capacity. And then her father and her uncle mixed cement and carefully patched the opening in the concrete by the light of a single lantern. After the cement set, they rubbed little bits of gravel into it to give it an aged appearance and they dusted it with dirt from the road so it would be the same shade as the rest of the porch cement.

Until then the Turks in Balikesir had been peaceful. But now, once they had heard of Ataturk's victory a hundred miles to the south, they suddenly grew courageous. The next morning they attacked, overrunning the Greeks and Armenians. They burned the Greek quarter to the ground and they butchered every Greek and Armenian they could find. The violence in Balikesir had not made the history books. Smyrna, sacked at the same time, overshadowed it, and I don't doubt that similar massacres were taking place in enough other Turkish cities to keep Balikesir out of the limelight.

Kitty's grandmother, however, had been only in Balikesir and had seen only what took place in Balikesir. She spoke calmly of it now. The burnings, the rape, the endless murder. Children pierced with swords, old men and women shot through the back of the head—screams, gunshots, blood, death.

She was one of the few to survive, but her words indicated that Kitty had been right: "I was young then, and pretty. And the Turks are animals. I was ravished. Can you believe this, to look at me now, that men would want to have me that way? And not just one man, no. But I was not killed. Everyone else in my family was killed, but I escaped. I was with a group of Greeks and an old Armenian man. We fled the city. We were on the roads for days. The old Armenian man died. It is funny, I cannot remember his name. We were crowded together aboard a ship. Then we were here, New York, America."

"And the gold?"

"Gone. The Turks must have it."

"Did they find it?"

"Not then, no. But they must have it now. It was years ago. And no Armenian went back for it. I was the only one of my family to live, and only the people of my family knew of the gold. So no Armenian found it, and so the Turks must have gotten it all."

Later Kitty said, "Damn you, why did you have to go and talk Armenian with her? I couldn't understand three words out of a hundred. If you think it's a picnic to sit listening to two people talk for hours and not catch a word—"

"She's a wonderful woman."

"She is, isn't she? You seemed interested in her story. Were you?"

"Very much."

"I'm glad. How on earth did you learn to speak the language, Evan? No, don't tell me. I don't even want to know. It made her whole day, though. She cornered me on the way out. Did you hear what she asked me?"

"No."

"She wanted to know if I was pregnant."

"Are you?"

"God, I hope not. I told her I wasn't, and she said I should get pregnant right away so that we would be married."

"She said that?"

"That's not all. She said you have a better chance to get pregnant if you keep your knees way up and stay that way as long as you can. She's a dirty old lady."

"She's grand."

"You're a dirty old man. Are you coming to the New Life tonight?"

"Around midnight."

"Good."

I took the subway back to my apartment and sat down at my typewriter and wrote up everything I could recall of Kitty's grandmother's story. I read through what I had written, then roamed the apartment, pulling books from the shelves, checking articles in various pamphlets and magazines. A broadside of the League for the Restoration of Cilician Armenia alluded to the confiscation of the wealth of the Armenians of Smyrna. But I could find no reference to the cache in Balikesir. Nothing at all.

A few days later the League was meeting on Attorney Street on the Lower East Side. The League meets once a month, and I go when I can. Sometimes a guest speaker discusses conditions in the Armenian Soviet Socialist Republic. Other times reports will be read from branches in other cities, other countries. Much of the time is devoted to general socializing, discus-

sions of the rug business, gossip. As far as I know, I'm
the only member who isn't Armenian. At the meeting
I looked up Nezor Kalichikian, who knows everyone
and everything and who, I knew, had lived in Smyrna.
We drank coffee and played a game of chess which he
won, as usual. I asked him about the gold of Smyrna.

"The Armenian treasure of Smyrna," he said solemnly. "What do you want to know about it?"

"What happened to it?"

He spread his small hands expressively. "What happened to everything? The Turks got it, of course. Since
they could not rape it or eat it or kill it or burn it, they
probably spent it. They couldn't have kept it long. They
managed to rid themselves of the Armenians and the
Greeks and the Jews, the only three groups in Turkey
who had the slightest idea how to manage money. Yes;
I know of the Armenian treasure. Are you really interested in this, Evan?"

"Yes."

"Any particular reason?"

"Some research I'm doing."

"Always research. Yes." He sipped his coffee. "The
Armenians pooled their wealth, you know. It was all
kept in gold. One did not keep money in paper bills in
those days. Not real money, not one's savings. Always
gold. The money was pooled and tucked away for safe-
keeping in a basement in Smyrna."

"In Smyrna?"

"Of course. And then the Turks must have taken it,
because no one succeeded in getting it out of the country. The whole city was burned, you understand. The
wretched Turkish quarter remained—that was the one
section that might have profited by a burning—but everything else was destroyed. Ataturk's troops fired the

city, and then, of course, they said that the Greeks and the Armenians had done it. Typical. I'm sure the gold was discovered during the fire. They looted everything."

"So they would have found the gold."

"Undoubtedly. If you move there, you'll lose your queen."

"Let it go, I moved it. Another game?"

"You resign?"

"Yes."

We set up the pieces for another game. Later he said, "There was an earthquake in Smyrna a few years after. Nineteen twenty-seven, I think."

"Nineteen twenty-eight."

"Perhaps. If the gold had not been found before, it would have been discovered then. So I'm sure the Turks have it."

"Would there have been much?"

"Oh, yes. Our people in Smyrna were quite wealthy, you know."

"And the gold was hidden right there in the city? In Smyrna?"

"Why, of course," old Nezor said. "Where else would it have been hidden?"

There were no records anywhere of the discovery of the treasure of Smyrna. It was taken for granted by everyone that the Turks had found the gold, but no one knew this for a certainty.

And there were no records anywhere to indicate that the gold had been cached in Balikesir. There was one woman's memory—and she claimed to be the only survivor who had known of the cache. Balikesir had not burned to the ground. Balikesir had not suffered an earthquake. Balikesir had suffered its private hells, but I could see a house on a hill, a porch with concrete sides and front, surviving through the years, its contents unknown and undisturbed.

That night I told Kitty. "I think it's still there," I said and explained it to her.

"Maybe it was never there in the first place. She's an old woman. She went through a big shock back then. Who knows what she remembers? Maybe she really lived in Smyrna all the time—"

"She wouldn't get something like that wrong. Nobody forgets the name of his home town."

"I suppose not. Evan—"

"Anything could have happened," I said. "The Turks could have found it, some Armenians could have known about it and gone back for it, the new owners of the house could have remodeled and found it, but still—"

"You think it's still there."

"I think it's possible."

"Would it be very much?"

"Figure that a British sovereign is worth ten or twelve dollars today. Figure they had about half the actual volume of the hiding place filled with gold. Judging by the size of the porch as she described it and just estimating roughly, yes, it would be a lot of money."

"How much?"

"I figured it out a little while ago. I can't really estimate it—hell, I don't really know that it's there or that it was ever there in the first place."

"How much?"

"A minimum of two million dollars. Possibly twice that much. Say three million dollars, maybe."

"Three million dollars," she said.

The next morning I went downtown and applied for a passport.

Chapter 4

It had all seemed magnificently simple then. I would fly to Istanbul and find some way of getting to Balikesir. I would work my way through the city—the present population is 30,000—until I found the house Kitty's grandmother had described to me. Her description was almost, but not quite, as good as a photograph. A very large house, three stories tall, on an elevation not far from the railroad station, and blessed with that extraordinary porch. There could not be too many houses of that description in Balikesir.

If I found the house, I would have to investigate to see if the porch was still intact, then provide myself with an elementary metals detector and determine if there was anything inside. And, if the gold was there, then it would be simply a matter of digging it out and taking it away. A difficult matter, no doubt, but one that could be puzzled out later.

It struck me as very likely that the gold was no longer there or had not been there in the first place. Still, one does not conclude that the grapes are sour without even attempting to see if the vine is within reach.

Three million dollars—

Just a portion of that wealth could do extraordinary things for the League for the Restoration of Cilician Armenia. Another chunk of gold would facilitate a vital worldwide direct-mail campaign for the Flat Earth Society. And more, and more. There was all that gold—perhaps—doing nothing for anyone, lying unattended and unknown, and here were all these marvelous groups able to make such good use of it.

So I had to go.

And it seemed such a facile matter, at least the first stages. I would go to Turkey and work things out from that point on. There was every reason to go and no particular reason not to. Cudahy's silly thesis was finished and would be accepted readily enough. I had completed my paper for the Jacobite Circle and mailed it off to their offices in Portree on the Isle of Skye. Most of all, I *wanted* to go. I feel that whenever possible one ought to do the things he wants to do.

How was I to know the damned Turks would arrest me?

Mustafa was poor company. He stayed with me like a summer cold and tried to shepherd me straight to the plane. I made for a newsstand and looked hungrily for something in English while Mustafa tugged at me. He could not have pried me loose with a crowbar. "Your mother was blinded by gonorrhea," I told him reasonably. "If you don't let me get something to read, I'll kill you."

The selection in English was dismal. There was a Turkish guidebook, a sort of anthropological sex manual by Margaret Mead, and four Agatha Christie mysteries. I bought everything but the Margaret Mead and let Mustafa get me onto the plane.

We sat in the tourist section. Evidently the Turkish Government intended to reroute spies as economically as possible. I had the middle seat between Mustafa and a fat schoolteacher—from Des Moines, I believe—who asked me at once if I was an American. I shook my head. She asked me if I spoke English, and I shook my head again. Then she put on her earphones and went to sleep.

The ride to Shannon was long, choppy, uncomfortable, and supremely dull. I was wedged between the sick-sweet lavender scent of the schoolteacher and the awesome pungence of Mustafa, who evidently had never been taught to bathe. I read the Turkish guidebook—there was hardly anything in it about Balikesir—and I read the four Agatha Christies. I'd read three of them before, but it didn't really matter. After nine days in that cell I'd have read the Johannesburg phone directory and enjoyed it.

The food was good, at least. It was tasteless, naturally, but there was a fairly large piece of some sort of beef on the tray, far more meat than I had had in nine days. There were also some plastic green peas and a crunchy green and purple salad. I ate everything but found myself missing the pilaff. I might never have pilaff like that again, I thought, and then I realized how I could contrive to eat that pilaff in the future. All I had to do was go to Turkey. I would be instantly arrested and instantly jailed, and I would be fed toast and pilaff and pilaff for the rest of my life.

Except, of course, that I would never be able to return to Turkey. The Turkish Government would revoke my visa and never grant another, and the U.S. Government would probably cancel my passport. It was unfair. I had done nothing. I had simply gone quietly and legally to Turkey, but they take people's passports away from them all the time. Which meant not only that I would not be able to go to Turkey again, but that I very possibly would not be able to go anywhere.

And throughout all of this there would be interrogation—endless interrogation. Why had I gone to Turkey? Who was I representing? What was I plotting? Who? What? Where? When? Why?

I have never liked being questioned. In all my sessions with the Federal Bureau of Investigation I have never enjoyed myself at all. I don't like having some competent young man sit down in my apartment and ask questions about my friends and my associations and my ideas and all of the rest.

But in each of these sessions—and there have been many of them—I have had one ultimate weapon. I have always told these officious oafs the truth. I have never lied to them. Since they cannot find any sense or logic in the way I live my life, and since I don't break their damned laws, they wind up going away and shaking their heads and clucking to themselves.

How could I tell them the truth now? How could I tell those people about the Armenian hoard?

No.

I simply could not return to the United States. I simply could not land in Washington.

I looked over at Mustafa. He had his earphones plugged into the wax in his ears and was listening, expressionless, to a medley of folk songs performed by the Norman Luboff Choir. If only there were a way of ridding myself of Mustafa, perhaps I had a chance to avoid returning to Washington. But how? Even if he dropped dead on the spot, if one of Norman Luboff's singers hit high C and burst a blood vessel in Mustafa's little brain, I was still stuck on the damned airplane. How could I pry him away from me, and how could I pry myself off the flight?

Shannon—

We would be landing at Shannon. Shannon Airport in Ireland. Not Turkey, not the United States of America. Ireland. And we would have two precious hours between planes. We would get off this plane, Mustafa and I, and we would wait in Shannon Airport for two hours before it was time to board our flight for Washington. I would have two hours to rid myself of Mustafa.

I almost shouted at the beauty of it. I knew people in Ireland! I received mail from Ireland every month; almost every week. I was an active member of the Clannna-Gaille and the Irish Republican Brotherhood. If I could find some of those people—any of them—I was safe. They would be my sort of people, my spiritual brothers. They would hide me, they would care for me, they would *conspire* with me!

Shannon—

I closed my eyes, tried to bring the map of Ireland into focus. Dublin in the center of the extreme right, Cork at the bottom, the Six Counties of Hibernia Irredenta at the top, Galway at the left. Below Galway, Shannon Airport. And near Shannon, what? Tralee? No, that was farther down and farther to the left. Now what was the city right near Shannon?

Limerick.

Of course, Limerick. And I knew someone in Limerick. I was sure I knew someone in Limerick. Who?

Francis Geoghan and Thomas Murphy lived in Dublin. P. T. Clancy lived in Howth, which was just north of Dublin, and Padraic Fynn lived in Dun Laoghaire, which was just south of Dublin, but there was someone in Limerick, and I merely had to remember his name.

Wait, now. Dolan? Nolan? I knew it, it was coming back, it only took thinking.

It was Dolan, P. P. Dolan, Padraic Pearse Dolan,

named for the greatest of the Easter Monday martyrs who had proclaimed the Irish Republic from the steps of the Post Office in O'Connell Street. And he didn't live in Limerick City but in County Limerick, and I remembered his whole address now: P. P. Dolan, Illanoloo, Croom, Co. Limerick, Republic of Ireland.

Where was Croom? It couldn't be far from Limerick itself. The whole county was not that large. If I reached him, he would hide me. He would welcome me and feed me and hide me.

If only I could get rid of Mustafa.

I looked at him, sitting contentedly while the music was piped into his ears. Dream on, I told him silently. You'll get yours, little man.

Istanbul is about 1,500 miles from Shannon. We made the trip in about three hours, and the time zones canceled out the flying time almost exactly. It had been close to four o'clock when we left Istanbul and it was about that time when we dropped through the cloud cover over Ireland.

I wasn't prepared for the greenness of it. The whole country is a brilliant green, cut up by piled-stone fences into patches of lime green and Kelly green and forest green, with thin swirling ribbons of gray road threading through the patchwork of green. There was a body of water topped with mist—the mouth of the Shannon? And there was green, miles and miles of green. I looked down at it, and something most unusual happened to me. All at once I was thinking in a rich brogue. All at once I was an Irishman and a member of the Irish Republican Brotherhood. It was my own home grounds we were coming to, and Mustafa did not have a chance.

We landed, taxied, stopped. I left my five books on the plane and walked at Mustafa's side into the small one-story airport. Our luggage had been checked through to Washington, so there was no real customs check. We stood in one short line, and a pleasant young man in a green uniform checked our passports. Mustafa handed both passports to him, and the man returned them, and Mustafa took them both and pocketed them. He seemed very pleased with himself. He had my passport, after all, so where could I go?

Indeed, where *could* I go? Mustafa led me to a bench, and the two of us sat side by side upon it. I looked around. There was a door that led to the Shannon Free Shopping Center, where one could buy things at ludicrous prices before departing. I hoped Mustafa would buy himself some scented soap. There was a booth where two beautiful, green-clad girls dispensed travel folders and sold tickets for the Bunratty Castle tour. There was a men's room. There were a pair of ticket counters for Pan Am and Aer Lingus, the Irish line. There was a ladies' room. There was a coffee bar. There was—

Of course!

I stood up. Mustafa rose to his feet at once and glared at me. "The men's room," I said. "The toilet. I have to use the toilet. I have to make a tinkle. I have to go potty, you idiot." He understood every word, of course, but we were both still pretending that he didn't. In desperation I pointed at the men's room door, then posed with my hands on my thighs and hunched forward in the classic Man Urinating posture.

"I can't go anywhere," I said. "You've got my bloody passport. Come along if you want."

And, of course, the little bastard came along.

The men's room was a long narrow affair. I walked the length of it, and my Turkish shadow stayed at my side. I paused in front of the last stall and asked him if he wanted to come in with me. He smiled and took up a position directly in front of the stall. I closed the door and bolted it.

So he thought I was James Bond, did he? Fine. Just for that I was going to.*be* James Bond.

I sat down on the throne and slipped my shoes off. I shrugged out of my jacket and hung it on the peg. I placed the shoes side by side, toes pointing outward, right where they would most likely be if I were doing what I had ostensibly come to do. I hoped Mustafa would be able to see the tips of the shoes.

Then I got down on my hands and knees and looked along the floor. The floor was immaculate, incidentally, so I knew at once that I was not in Turkey. There was one stall occupied about halfway down. I waited hopefully, and a toilet flushed, and a man got to his feet and left. The outer door swung shut behind him.

Now—

I crawled under the partition, around the next toilet, under the next partition, around still another toilet, into another stall, all the way down to the end. I did this as quickly and as silently as possible, squirming on my belly like a pit viper, and certain that I was going much too slowly and making far too much noise.

I was in the very last stall when I heard the outside door open. I stopped breathing. A man came in, used the urinal, left. I wondered if Mustafa was still standing there like a soldier. I peeked out at him, and there he was, a cigarette dangling from his lower lip, his eyes focused stupidly upon my shoes.

At first I was going to slip out the door and run. But

how far would I get? I'd have a two-minute jump on him at the most, and I'd be running all over Ireland in my socks. No, it wouldn't do. I had to nail him and I had to get my shoes back.

I slipped out of the stall, lowered my head and charged.

He barely moved at all. At the last moment he turned lazily around just in time to see me hurtling through the air at him. His mouth fell open, and he started to take a small step backward, and I sailed into him, my head ramming him in the pit of his soft stomach, and down we went.

I was ready for a war. I had visions of us bouncing one another off plumbing fixtures, hurling karate chops at one another, fighting furiously until one of us managed to turn the tide. But this was not to be. I had never realized just how great an advantage surprise can provide. Mustafa collapsed like a blown tire. We fell in a heap, and I landed on top, and he did nothing but gape at me.

I was drunk with power. I clapped a hand over his foul mouth and leaned all my weight upon his chest and stomach. "My mother, who died some years ago, never had anything to do with dogs or camels," I said in much better Turkish than his own. "You are a foul pig to suggest such a thing." And I gave his head a tentative bang on the tile floor.

"You are also doomed," I said. "I'm a secret agent working for the establishment of a free and independent Kurdistan. I've poisoned the entire water supply of Istanbul. Within a month everyone in Turkey will perish of cholera."

His eyes rolled in his head.

"Sleep well," I said, and I slammed his head against

the floor again, but infinitely harder this time. His eyes went glassy, and their lids flopped shut, and for a moment I was afraid that I had actually gone and killed him. I checked his pulse. He was still alive.

I dragged him back into the stall where I'd left my shoes and jacket and I stripped off all his clothes and used strips of his shirt to tie him up and gag him. I tied his hands together behind his back and lashed his feet together and propped him up on the toilet seat. He wasn't stirring at all, and I guessed that he would stay out for quite some time. I locked the door so that no one would disturb him in the meanwhile, put on my own shoes and jacket, made a little bundle of his remaining clothing, and crawled into the adjoining compartment with it. Then I walked out of the men's room.

I took my passport and Mustafa's passport from his pants and put them both in my pocket. I stuffed his clothes in a trash can and poked them down to the bottom. I kept expecting him to emerge from the men's room and chase after me, but he stayed where he was, and I hurried through a pair of big glass doors to the outside.

No air was ever fresher. It had begun to rain, a fine misty rain, and the air had a sharp chill. My summer suit, ideal for Istanbul, was not the right thing at all for Ireland. I didn't care. I was out of Turkey and out of Mustafa's hands and free, and I could barely believe it.

There were taxis, but I didn't dare take one. Someone might remember me. I couldn't leave a trail. I asked an Aer Lingus stewardess where I could get a bus to Limerick. She pointed at an oldish double-decker bus, and I headed toward it.

"You've forgotten your luggage," she called after me.

"I'm leaving it at the airport."

I got onto the bus and went up to the top. We waited five very long minutes. Then the bus pulled out onto a narrow road and headed for Limerick. After a few moments a conductor came upstairs and collected the fare from everyone. It was five shillings. He came to me and looked at my suit and asked for seventy cents. I gave him a dollar bill, and he took a long limp ticket, punched it in several places, gave it to me, and handed me a two-shilling piece and two large copper pennies in change.

We drove a mile. Then we slowed to a stop, and I saw a uniformed man wearing a pistol emerge from a glassed-in shack and board the bus. My heart jumped. Mustafa had gotten out, he had called ahead, they were looking for me—

I looked at the man across the aisle from me. "Please," I said, "do you know why they've stopped us?"

"Customs check," he said. "It's just the garda seeing that no one's bringing something in from the free shopping center."

"They always do this?"

"They do."

I thanked him and tried to remain calm. Mustafa could not possibly have escaped yet, I told myself. He was probably still out cold. And even if he got loose, he would be a while figuring out how to burst stark naked upon the Irish scene without creating an uproar. And with no passport and no identification at all he might be in almost as much trouble as I was. So I ought to have a few hours' start, but still I wished I didn't have to look at any men in uniforms.

The garda climbed the stairs and walked the length of the aisle. Did anyone have anything to declare? No one did. He repeated the question in Gaelic, and still no one had anything to declare. He started toward the stairs again and then he stopped beside me, and I froze.

"American, are you?"

I managed a nod.

He touched my suit. "Fine cloth," he said, "but if you'll permit me, sir, you might be finding it a bit thin for Ireland. Perhaps you'll buy yourself a good Irish jacket."

Somehow I smiled at him. "I'll do that," I said. "Thank you."

"Thank you, sir," he said and left, and the bus started up again. Some moments after that I began to breathe almost normally.

Chapter 5

I left the bus in what I judged to be the center of Limerick City. The main business street was clean and neat and modest. It bustled with cars and cyclists, and I had difficulty crossing it. The traffic kept to the left, of course, and I kept wanting to look the wrong way as I stepped off the curb. An old woman on a bicycle very nearly ran me down.

The chill misty rain was still falling, and both the bus driver and the garda had noticed my suit and identified me at once as an American. I found a clothing shop and ducked inside. The clerk was tall and slender and young and black-haired, with the ascetic face of a seminarian. He was just about to close for the night. I bought a pair of gray woolen trousers and a bulky, tweed sport coat that must have weighed far more in pounds than the eight it cost. I added a black wool sweater and a checked cloth cap. The whole bill came to fourteen pounds and change, something like forty dollars.

"I have only American money," I said.

"Oh, I'm very sorry," he said.

"You can't accept it?"

"Oh, I can, but the banks are closed, sir. I'll have to charge you a sixpence on the pound for changing it."

I gave him a hundred dollars, and he computed everything very carefully with paper and pencil, then gave me my change in a mixture of English and Irish notes. He wrapped up my American suit very carefully with brown paper secured with heavy twine. He had thanked me when I made each of my selections and when I passed him the money. He thanked me once more when he gave me my change and again as he returned my wrapped suit. He grinned impishly as I stood with it under my arm.

"You look Irish now," he said.

"Do I?" I was pleased.

"You do. Good day, sir. And"—inevitably—"thank you."

I found a small dark pub on the side street. I was the only customer at the bar. A group of older men—all, I noted gladly, dressed in heavy sweaters and tweed sport coats and cloth caps—sat drinking Guinness and playing dominoes in a room off to the side. A woman poured me a stemmed glass of Irish whiskey and set a pitcher of water alongside it.

"Is it far to Croom?" I asked.

"Not far. Perhaps ten miles. Are you for Croom, sir?"

"I thought I might go there, yes."

"Have you a car?"

"No, I haven't. I thought I might take a bus. Is there a bus that goes to Croom?"

"There is, but I don't think there will be another to-night for Croom." She turned toward the domino game. "Sean? Is there a bus tonight for Croom?"

"Not until morning. It leaves at eight-thirty from the station near the Treaty Stone." To me he said, "It's to Croom you want to go, sir?"

"Yes."

"There's a bus in the morning, but none before. Could you wait until morning?"

By morning they would be combing Limerick for their escaped spy. "I hoped to go tonight," I said.

"It's not hard walking if you don't mind the rain. It would take you two hours, less than that if you're a good walker. Or you could rent a cycle for half a crown for the day. Mulready's will rent you one and give you good directions in the bargain. You'd be in Croom in less than an hour."

"Perhaps I'll do that."

"You're from America, are you?"

"Yes, I am."

"It's your first trip to Ireland?"

"Yes." And because a rushed visit to a hamlet seemed to require some explanation, I added, "I have an aunt in Croom. She was going to send someone to Limerick to pick me up in the morning, but I thought I'd go tonight to surprise her and save someone a trip."

"Did you want to start right away?"

"As soon as I can. I haven't been on a bike . . . a cycle in years. I'd rather not try an unfamiliar road in the dark."

"Mulready would see you got one with a good head-lamp. But you'd do well to start soon. If you'd care to walk with me"—he stood up from his domino game—"it's not far, and I'm headed that way myself, so I could take you to Mulready's shop."

It was, I was sure, very much out of his way; I had no doubt that he had planned to sit at his domino game for several more hours. But there seemed no way to refuse such graciousness. I managed to buy a round of drinks for the house, and then Sean insisted on buying one back. I was feeling the drinks as we walked through

the rain down one street and over another, each nar-
rower than the last. Sean wanted to talk about America.
He had family in New York and Philadelphia and he
thought John Kennedy might have saved the world had
he lived a few years longer.

I gave my name as Michael Farrell and said I was
from Boston. There were Farrells throughout County
Limerick, he assured me, and surely many of them
were my relatives.

John Mulready was in his bicycle shop, a dark and
cluttered little establishment between a butcher shop
and a tobacconist on a narrow street. Sean introduced
me as a visitor from America come to stay with relatives in Croom, and could Mulready rent me a cycle for
the trip? He could. And could he provide me with directions? He could, and with pleasure. I thanked Sean,
and he thanked me, and we shook hands briskly, and he
went back out into the rain.

Mulready was thick-bodied, florid-faced and fif-
tyish, with a brogue I had trouble understanding. He
brought out a large cycle with a huge headlamp and an
array of wires running here and there. He suggested I
get up on it and see if it seemed the right size. I lifted
myself gingerly onto the bicycle and wondered if I
would be able to ride the thing. I told him I hadn't been
on a cycle in years.

He was surprised. "Do they not have cycles in America, then?"

"Only for the children."

He shook his head in wonder. "Who would have
thought it? The richest country in the universe, and
only the children may have cycles. Who would believe
it possible?"

I asked him how much deposit he required. He didn't

seem to understand, and I thought at first that he was having trouble catching the word, or that *deposit* was not the correct term in Ireland. It turned out that he recognized the word but not the concept. Why on earth would he care to take a deposit from me? Was I not a friend of Sean Flynn and would I not return the cycle when I had finished with it?

I asked the price. Two-and-six a day, he said, and less if I kept it a full week. I told him I'd need it for several days at least and reached for my money. He insisted that I pay him when I returned to save keeping records.

He told me the way to find the road to Croom and how to follow it. "You begin on the road to Adare and Rathkeale and Killarney, but you'll come first to Patrickswell and just past Patrickswell you'll turn south, and that will be on your left as you go. There will be a sign saying Croom so that you won't miss it. It's a good road, it is, paved all the way, and no more than ten or twelve miles from here to Croom."

I told him I had the directions down pat. He repeated them, and insisted on drawing a rudimentary map for me to take along. I thanked him again, and he suggested that perhaps he might accompany me as far as the edge of the city so that I would get off on the right foot. I told him it was kind of him, but I was sure I would be all right. His expression suggested that he doubted this but was too polite to say so. He asked me how I liked Ireland. I said that I liked the country very much and that the people seemed to be the finest on earth. We shook hands warmly on that, and I wheeled my cycle out to the street and clambered onto it, hoping I wouldn't fall off at once and that he wouldn't see me if I did.

*   *   *

Cycling, I discovered, is like swimming; once learned, it is never wholly forgotten. The bike was unfamiliar and awkward for me. I seemed to be sitting too far off the ground and I had a bad time at first remembering that one braked by squeezing the metal gadgets on the handlebars. I kept trying to brake by reversing the direction of the pedals, which was how one accomplished the process when I was a boy—and how odd that I remembered it. And once I squeezed the handbrake accidentally, and the cycle stopped suddenly, and I did not. I flew from the cycle, the cap flew from my head, and a red Volkswagen had to swerve hard to the right to avoid demolishing the cycle and me.

But by the time I was out of Limerick City I had gotten the hang of it again. And then, with nothing to do but pedal the bike endlessly onward, with nothing to look at but green fields darkening in the twilight and occasional smooth stone huts with thatched roofs, with no greater hurdle than the occasional sheep and pigs that wandered about in the road and gazed into the cycle's headlamp, the whole hysterical madness of my situation came home to me. The reality of it had vanished in Limerick. The clothing store, the pub, the bicycle shop—each had provided conversation and warmth and motions to go through, words to say, a role to be played and lived with. There had been relatively little time to waste in thought.

Now, on an empty road to Croom, I had time to realize that my actions in the Shannon Airport men's room had been not those of James Bond but of a madman. I had escaped, but from what? A flight to my own country, a round of unpleasant but harmless questions put by the unpleasant but harmless agents of the Federal Bureau of Investigation, a possible loss of my passport (which action I could certainly appeal and probably overcome), and the impossibility of returning to Turkey for a shot at the cache of gold.

And now what had I accomplished? I had committed no crime to begin with and had very definitely committed one in escaping. I was like the innocent man who shoots the policeman who had been trying to arrest him by mistake. My original innocence had been entirely washed out. By now the U.S. Government would be very concerned about getting hold of me, and the Turks would be anxious to learn more of me, and the Irish police would be preparing to capture me. I could not go back to the States, I could not go back to Turkey, and I could not stay safely in Ireland. I was cold, I was starving, I was being rained upon, and I was getting cramps in my legs from pedaling the damned cycle up and down more damned hills than I had known existed.

Why should P. P. Dolan waste a minute on me? Why should he offend at least three governments by giving aid and comfort to a spy? And when I called myself a member of the Brotherhood, suppose he was a turncoat, an informer? I pictured Victor McLaglen hulking in the doorway of a thatched hut. What would he do for me? Nothing. What *could* he do for me? Nothing.

I hit a stone and fell off the bicycle. By now, I thought, dragging myself to my feet and hauling the cycle to an upright position, by now I would be snug in the belly of a Pan American jet bound for Washington. In a few hours I would be explaining the foolishness of the situation to a pleasant young agent with a crew cut and a firm handshake. We would laugh together about the vagaries of the Turkish Government and the absurdity of our suspicion-ridden world. He would buy me a drink, I would buy him a drink, we would sit in a bar somewhere warm and dry, and in the morning, after a full evening of drunken camaraderie, I would take a train back to New York and my apartment and my books and my projects and my societies and my Kitty.

I mounted the bike and pressed onward.

I reached and passed the town of Patrickswell—a scattering of small shops, a church, a few dozen cottages. I seemed to have been riding forever. It was darker now, and the rain was coming down harder than before. I reached the fork in the road that pointed me toward Croom. I had been sure I would miss it, but I swung to the left and headed into a long downhill stretch that gave me a chance to stop pedaling, relax, and coast a while. I wished that I had stopped in Patrickswell for a drink and a bite to eat. I wished I had stayed in a pub in Limerick until it stopped raining, if it ever did stop raining in Ireland. I wished that the Irish Republican Brotherhood would do something about the damned rain. I wished I was on the plane for Washington.

Croom was small and silent, a nest of cottages, a two-story hotel, a block of storefronts in the center of town. I parked my cycle in front of a pub and went inside. It seemed to be a grocery store as well as a pub. There were two men at the bar drinking whiskey and another man behind the bar sipping beer. I had a drink of John Jameson. The three were talking in Gaelic.

In English I asked the bartender if he knew where P. P. Dolan lived.

He gave me tortuous directions. It seemed impossible that so small a town could hold a house so difficult to reach. I thanked him and went outside. The drink was making my head swim, and when I mounted the cycle again I didn't think I would be able to ride at all.

The few minutes in the pub had been just enough time for my legs to knot up completely.

I followed the directions, made all the correct turns, and found the house. It was a small cottage, gray in the dim light. A television antenna perched on the thatched roof, and smoke trickled upward from the chimney.

I staggered to the door, hesitated, tried to catch my breath, failed, and rapped on the door. I heard footsteps, and the door was drawn open. I looked at the little man in the doorway and remembered the Victor McLaglen I had visualized. This man was more a leprechaun, short, gnarled, with piercingly blue eyes.

"P. P. Dolan?"

"I am."

"Padraic Pearse Dolan?"

He seemed to straighten up. "Himself."

"You've got to help me," I said. The words flowed in a torrent. "I'm from America, from New York, I'm a member of the Brotherhood—the Irish Republican Brotherhood—and they're after me. I was in jail. I escaped when we reached Ireland. You have to hide me." And, gasping for breath, I dug out my passport and handed it to him.

He took it, opened it, looked at it, at me, at it again. "I don't understand," he said gently. "The picture's no likeness of you at all. And it says that your name is . . . let me see"—he squinted in the half light—"Mustafa Ibn Ali. Did I say that properly?"

Chapter 6

If you'll come inside and sit by the fire, Mr. Ali," the little man was saying. "It's cold outside, and so damp. And would you take a cup of tea, Mr. Ali? Nora, if you would be fixing Mr. Ali a cup of tea. Now, Mr. Ali—"

I had made two mistakes, it seemed. When I changed my summer suit for proper Irish clothing, I had transferred only one passport and the wrong one at that. My own passport remained in my suit. And my suit, so carefully wrapped by the young clerk, had somehow been separated from me. I had carried the parcel into the pub, but I hadn't had it with me when I left Mulready's cycle shop. I'd left it either at the pub or with Mulready, suit and passport and all.

"My name's not Mr. Ali," I said. "I took his passport by mistake. He's a Turk. He was my jailer in Turkey. He was taking me back to America when I escaped."

"You were a prisoner, then?"

"Yes." His face seemed troubled by this, so I added, "It was political, my imprisonment."

This eased his mind considerably. Nora, his daughter, came over to us with the tea. She was a slender thing, small-boned, almost dainty, with milk-white skin and glossy black hair and clear blue eyes. "Your tea, Mr. Ali," she said.

"It's not his name after all," her father said. "And what would your name be, sir?"

"Evan Tanner."

"Tanner," he said. "Forgive me if I seem to pry, Mr. Tanner, but what led you to come here? To Croom and to my house?"

I told him a bit of it. He became quite excited at the thought that I was an American member of the Brotherhood and that I had heard of him. "Do they know of me, then, in America?" he mused. "And who would have guessed it?"

But it was Nora who seized on my name. "Evan Tanner. Evan Michael Tanner, is it?"

"Yes, that's right—"

"You know him, Nora?"

"If it's the same," she said. "And Mr. Tanner, is it you who writes articles in *United Irishmen?* Oh, you know him, Da. In last month's paper, the article suggesting that honorary representatives of the Six Counties be given seats in the Dail. 'Wanted: Representation for Our Northern Brethren,' by Evan Michael Tanner, and wasn't it the article you admired so much, and saying what a grand idea it was, and wouldn't you like to shake the hand of the man that wrote it?"

He looked wide-eyed at me. "And was it you who wrote that article, Mr. Tanner?"

"It was."

He took the tea from me. "Nora," he said, "spill this out. Bring the jar of Power's. And hurry over to Garrity's and fetch your brother Tom. I only wish my eldest son could be here, Mr. Tanner, for it's glad he'd be to meet you, a faithful member of the Brotherhood that he is, but the poor lad's in England now."

"Not in jail, I hope."

"No, praise God, but working in an office there. For what can a young man do to earn his keep in this god-forsaken country? Go quickly, Nora, and bring Tom back with you. And mind who you tell!" He shook his head sadly. "It's a hell of a thing to say," he explained, "but there are spies and informers everywhere."

The four of us, Dolan and Nora and Tom and I, listened to the latest developments in the Evan Tanner case on the kitchen radio. It seemed that Mustafa had seen a good number of James Bond movies, and they had served to supplement his account of my escape. According to the radio report, I was a dangerous spy of unknown allegiance being returned to America after attempting to infect all of Turkey with a plague of cholera. In the Shannon lavatory I had crushed a small pellet between my fingers, liberating a gas that temporarily paralyzed Mustafa's spinal column. Though he fought valiantly, he was in no condition to prevent my knocking him unconscious and trussing him up.

It was assumed that I had taken refuge in Limerick. The gardai were presently combing Limerick City, their numbers reinforced by a special detachment of plain-clothes detectives sent up from Dublin, and an arrest would no doubt be made in a matter of hours.

"It looks bad," I said. "Sooner or later they'll turn up the suit and spot the passport. Once they trace me to the bicycle shop, Mr. Mulready will be able to tell them that I went to Croom. And if they follow me this far, they'll be sure to find me."

"You're safe here," Dolan said.

"If the gardai come—"

"This house has been searched before," Dolan said. He drew himself up very straight. "Many times by the

Tans and often enough by the Free State troops during the Civil War. Why, didn't my father hide half the Limerick Flying Column here? And when Michael Flaherty and the Dwyer boy did for that British lorry outside of Belfast, wasn't it here that they came? And hid in the upstairs room for three weeks before they got the boat for America. There's many a man on the run who's hid in Dolan's house, and never a one of them that's been taken. Nora will fix the attic room for you. You'll be comfortable enough in the bed, and the gardai could search this house ten times over and never set eyes on you."

"I couldn't let you take such a risk—"

"Don't talk nonsense. And don't be worrying about your suit, either. Most likely it's still in Mulready's, waiting for you to come back for it. If you left it there, it's still there now. And if you left it in the pub, sure they'll take it to Mulready's, knowing you'll have to return to the cycle shop sooner or later. Tom can go for it tomorrow, and you'll have it in your hands without the gardai ever knowing of it."

"If they're already there and see him—"

"Tom will be looking for them, and if they're there, he will leave without being seen. Don't bother yourself about it, Mr. Tanner. But sit back, you must be tired. Are you after getting to bed right away or would you sit a while first?"

I said I would sooner sit and talk with him. Tom put a few more cakes of turf on the fire, and Nora freshened our drinks. She asked if I had been born in America, and I said I had, and she asked what part of Ireland my parents had lived in.

"Actually," I admitted, "I'm not Irish."

"In the Brotherhood and not an Irishman!"

My explanation filled them with wonder. Padraic

Pearse Dolan got solemnly to his feet and stood gazing into the fire. "I've often said it," he said. "That men of goodwill throughout the world will rally to our cause, whether or not they be Irish. There are many demonstrations for the restoration of the Six Counties in America, are there not? The young people, the college students, with their marching and their picket signs?"

"But isn't that mostly for Vietnam?" Nora asked. "And civil rights and the hydrogen bomb?"

"Vietnam, civil rights, bombs, and Ireland—all one and the same," Dolan said. "It's that the whole world is Irish in spirit, wouldn't you say as much, Mr. Tanner?"

I agreed with this, and Nora filled our glasses again, and Tom took a harmonica from his pocket and began to play "The Boys From Wexford." He was short and slender around nineteen or twenty, a few years younger than his sister and graced with the same dark good looks. We spent hours in front of the fire, finishing one jar of whiskey and tapping into a second, talking, singing, trading stories. Dolan had seen fighting, himself, on two occasions, against the Free State forces in 1932 and in the north a few years later. The earlier engagement had been the more heroic. He was only fifteen at the time and he lay in ambush with four lads not much older than himself. They trapped two Free State soldiers on a road near Ennis in County Clare and gunned them down. One was in the hospital for nearly a month, he said, and the other walks with a limp to this day. In the north they had lobbed six Mills bombs into a British post office. None had exploded, one of Dolan's group had two fingers of his left hand shot off, and the lot of them wound up spending six months in Dartmoor.

"Bloody British jail," he said. "What fine breakfasts

they served us, though! You'd never get a breakfast like that in Ireland. Two slices of gammon and three eggs."

Nora sang "Danny Boy" in a high willowy voice that had us all crying, and I taught them a group of songs from the Rebellion of 1798 that not one of them had heard before. I told Dolan I'd learned them from a Folkways record and that they were traditional.

"Never heard a one of them," he said.

"They're folk music," I explained. "Handed down by the countryfolk from one generation to the next."

"Then that explains it," he said.

And midway through the second jar of whiskey I began talking about Turkey and why I had gone there. No one had asked; they had simply taken it for granted that I was a fine boy, that the Turks were heathens, and that any government with an unhealthy interest in me was surely in the wrong and thus merely illustrated the malevolence of officialdom. When I told of the fortune in Armenian gold their eyes went wide, and Nora sighed in amazement and shivered beside me.

"You'll have your fortune," Dolan pronounced. "You'll be wealthy, with acres of land and a house like a castle."

"I don't want the money for myself."

"Are you daft? You—"

I explained about the causes that had need of money. He seemed utterly astonished that I intended to endow, among several other worthy groups, the Irish Republican Army.

"You'll want to think that over," he said. "What would those bloody fools do with so much gold? They'd be after blowing up all of Belfast, and all be getting into trouble."

"They might regain the six counties," I said.

"Ah," he sighed, and his eyes took on a faraway look. "You're a fine boy, Evan. And it is a grand thing you would do."

I hadn't planned to talk about the gold, and if they had asked me I would probably have invented some convenient lie. But no one did ask, and so there was no reason to hide the truth. Besides, I almost had to talk about it now to make it at all real for myself. There in that cozy hut, with those fine warm people, there was no Turkey, no gold, no Mustafa, no toast and pilaff and pilaff. Only the rich singing of untrained off-key voices, and the warmth of roasting peat and peat-smoked whiskey, and the close sweet beauty of Nora.

When his father dozed off in front of the fire Tom Dolan showed me to my room. It was reached through a trapdoor in the second-floor ceiling. Tom stood on a chair, moved a lever, and a flap dropped from the ceiling, releasing a rope ladder. I followed Tom up the ladder and into a long, narrow room. The ceiling, less than four feet high in the center, sloped to meet the floor on either side. A mattress in the center of the room was piled generously high with quilts and blankets. Tom lit a candle at the side of it and said he hoped I wasn't the sort who grew nervous in cramped quarters.

"To shut up tight," he said, "you haul in the ladder and then catch hold of that ring in the panel with the stick. Draw it shut and fasten it, you see, and it cannot be opened from below. And no one would think there's a room up here, with so little space and no window. Will you be all right here?"

"It seems comfortable."

"Oh, it is. I'd be here myself, and you in my bed, but Da wouldn't allow it. He says you must be secure if the gardai come." He hesitated. "How is it in America, Mr. Tanner?"

"Evan."

"Do they pay good wages there? And are jobs to be had? My brother Jamie's been after me to come to London, but what I've heard of America—"

"Don't you want to stay in Ireland?"

"She's the finest country in the world, and the finest people in it. But a man ought to see something of the world. And there's not such an abundance of things to occupy a younger man in Croom. Unless one's a priest or a drunkard. I'm nineteen now, and I'll be out of here before I'm twenty-one, God willing."

He clambered back down the rope ladder and tossed it up to me, then raised the panel so that I could catch it with the hooked stick. I locked myself in, blew out the candle, and stretched out on my mattress in the darkness. It was still raining, and I could hear the rain on the thatched roof.

I was tired, and my body ached from the cycling. I went through the Hatha Yoga relaxation ritual, relaxing groups of muscles in turn by tightening them and letting them relax all the way. When this was completed I did my deep, measured, breathing exercises. I concentrated on an open white circle on a field of black, picturing this symbol in my mind and thinking of nothing else. After about half an hour I let myself breathe normally, yawned, stretched, and got up from the mattress.

I went downstairs. The turf fire still burned in the hearth. I sat in front of it and let myself think of the gold in Balikesir. My mind was clearer now, and I felt a good deal better physically, with the effects of the whiskey almost completely worn off.

It's difficult to remember what sleep was like or how

I used to feel upon awakening; sensory memory is surprisingly short-lived. I do not believe, though, that sleep (in the days when I slept) ever left me as refreshed as twenty minutes or an hour of relaxation does now.

The gold. Obviously I had gone about things the wrong way. It would now be necessary to approach the whole situation through the back door, so to speak. I would stay in Ireland just long enough for the manhunt for the notorious Evan Michael Tanner to cool down a bit. Then I would leave Ireland and work my way through continental Europe and slip into Turkey over the Bulgarian border. I would set up way stations along the route, men I could trust as I had trusted P. P. Dolan.

Europe was filled with such men. Little men with special schemes and secret dark hungers. And I knew these men. Without asking an eternity of questions, without demanding that I produce a host of documents, they would do what they had to do, slipping me across borders and through cities, easing me into Turkey and out again.

Was it fantastic? Of course. Was it more fantastic than lying on a mattress between the ceiling and the thatched roof of an Irish cottage? No, not really.

I was, I thought, rather like a runaway slave bound for Canada, following the drinking gourd north, stopping at the way stations of the Underground Railway. It could be managed, I realized. It needed planning, but it could be managed.

I was so lost in planning that I barely heard her footsteps on the stairs. I turned to her. She was wearing a white flannel wrapper and had white slippers upon her tiny feet.

"I knew you were down here," she said. "Is it difficult for you to sleep up there?"

"I wasn't tired. I hope I didn't wake you?"

"I could not sleep myself. No, you were quiet, I didn't hear you, but I thought that you were down here. Shall I build the fire up?"

"Not on my account."

"Will you have tea? Oh, and are you hungry? Of course you are. What you must think of us, pouring jars of punch into you and giving you nothing to eat. Let me fry you a chop."

"Oh, don't bother."

"It's no bother." She made a fresh pot of tea and fried a pair of lean lamb chops and a batch of potatoes. We ate in front of the fire and afterward sat with fresh cups of tea. She asked me what I was going to do. I told her some of the ideas that had been going through my mind, ways of getting back into Turkey.

"You'll really go, then."

"Yes."

"It must be grand to be able to go places, just to go and do things. I was going to take the bus to Dublin last spring, but I never did. It's just stay home and cook for Da and Tom and care for the house. It's only a few hours to Dublin by bus. Can you ever go back to your own country, Evan?"

"I don't know," I said slowly.

"For if you're in trouble there—"

"I hadn't even thought of that. I can't go back now, but when it all blows over—"

"You could stay in Ireland, though." Her eyes were very serious. "I know you're after getting the gold now, but when you've taken the treasure and escaped with it, why, if you couldn't get back to America, you could always come to Ireland."

"I don't think the Irish Government cares too much for me just now."

"Sure, you're a ten-day wonder, but they'll forget you. And anyone can get into Ireland. It's getting out of Ireland that everyone's after, you know. You could come back."

I realized, suddenly, that she had put on perfume. She had not been wearing any scent earlier in the evening. It was a very innocent sort of perfume, the type a mother might buy her daughter when she wore her first brassiere.

"Are you a Catholic, Evan?"

"No."

"A Protestant, then."

"No. I don't have a religion exactly."

"Then, if you wanted to, you could become a Catholic?"

"If I wanted to."

"Ah."

"I thought of it once. A very good friend of mine, a priest, made a fairly heroic effort to convert me. It didn't take."

"But that's not to say it couldn't some other time, is it?"

"Well, I don't think—"

She put her hand on mine. "You *could* come back to Ireland," she said slowly, earnestly. "Not saying that you will or won't, but you *could*. And you *could* turn Catholic, though not saying will or won't." Her cheeks were pink now, her eyes bluer than ever in the firelight. "It's a sin all the same, but not so serious, you know. And if Father Daly hears my confession, instead of Father O'Neill, he won't be so hard on me. Ah, Nora, hear yourself! Talking of the confession and penance before the sin itself, and isn't that a sin of another sort!"

We kissed. She sighed gratefully and set her head

on my chest. I ran a hand through her black hair. She raised her head and our eyes met.

"Tell me lies, Evan."

"Perhaps I'll come back to Ireland, and to Croom."

"Ahhh!"

"And perhaps, God willing, I'll find my faith."

"You're the sweetest liar. Now one more lie. Who do you love?"

"I love you, Nora."

We crawled through the trapdoor to my little crow's nest between ceiling and roof. I retrieved the ladder and the panel and closed us in. No one would hear us, she assured me. Her father and brother slept like the dead, and sounds did not carry well in the cottage.

She would not let me light the candle. She took off her robe in a corner of the room, then crept to my side and joined me under all the quilts and blankets. We told each other lies of love and made them come true in the darkness.

There had, I found, been other liars before me, a discovery that filled me at once with sorrow and relief.

Afterward she slept, but only for a few moments. I held her in my arms and drew the covers over us both. When she awoke she touched my face, and we kissed.

"A tiny sin," she said, not very seriously this time.

"Hardly a sin at all."

"And if I'd been born to be perfect, they'd surely have put me away in a convent, and then who would care for Da?"

She left me, found her robe, opened the trapdoor, and started down the ladder. "Now," she said, "now you'll sleep."

Chapter 7

In the hours before breakfast I read a popular biography of Robert Emmet and several chapters from *The Lives of the Saints*. Around five-thirty I stepped outside the cottage. A mist was rising from the countryside and melting under the glow of false dawn. The air had a damp chill to it. It was not raining, but it felt as though it might start again at any moment.

A few minutes past six Nora came down and started breakfast. She wore a skirt and sweater and looked quite radiant. Her father and brother followed a few minutes later. We ate sausages and eggs and toast and drank strong tea.

Before long I was alone again. Tom had gone to return the bicycle and retrieve my suit and passport, Nora was off for church and then a round of shopping, and Dolan had left to join a crew mending a road south of the town. I sat down with a pad of notepaper and a handful of envelopes and began writing a group of cryptic letters. It would be well, I felt, to leave as soon as possible and it would probably not be a bad idea if some of my prospective hosts on the continent had a vague idea that they were about to have a clandestine house guest on their hands. I couldn't be sure what route I might take, what borders would be hard to cross or where I would be unwelcome, so I wrote more letters than I felt

I could possibly need. The intended recipients ranged as far geographically as Spain and Latvia, as far politically as a Portuguese anarcho-syndicalist and a brother and sister in Roumania who hoped to restore the monarchy. I didn't expect to see a quarter of them, but one never knew.

I made the letters as carefully vague as I could. Some of my prospective hosts lived in countries where international mail was opened as a matter of course, and others in more open nations lived the sort of lives that made their governments inclined to deny them the customary rights of privacy. The usual form of my letters ran rather like this:

> Dear Cousin Peder,
>
> *It is my task to tell you that my niece Kristin is celebrating the birth of her first child, a boy. While I must travel many miles to the christening, I have the courage to hope for a warm welcome and shelter for the night.*
>
> *Faithfully,*
> *Anton*

The names and phrasing were changed, of course, to fit the nationality of the recipient and the language of each letter was the language of the person to whom it was sent. I finished the last one, sealed them all and addressed as many envelopes as I could. I couldn't remember all the addresses but knew I could learn most of the ones I was missing in London. Almost all my groups have contacts in London.

I couldn't mail the letters from Croom, of course,

and wasn't sure whether or not it would be safe to mail them all from the same city, anyway. But at least they were written.

When Nora came back to the cottage she kept blushing and turning from me. "I'm to have nothing to do with you," she said.

"All right, then."

"Must you accept it so readily?"

I laughed and reached for her. She danced away, blue eyes flashing merrily, and I lunged again and fell over my own feet. She hurried over to see if I was all right, and I caught her and drew her down and kissed her. She said I was a rascal and threw her arms around me. We broke apart suddenly when there was a noise outside, and the door flew suddenly open. It was Tom. His cycle—or mine, or Mr. Mulready's—was in a heap at the doorstep.

"Mr. Tanner fell down," Nora began, "and I was seeing whether he'd broken any bones, and—"

Tom only had time for one quick doubting look at her. He was out of breath, and his face was streaked with perspiration. "The old woman at the pub found your suit," he said. "Went to the gardai. They traced you to Mulready, and the fool said you were bound for Croom, and there's a car of them on the road from Limerick. I passed them coming back."

"You passed them?"

"I did. They had a flat tire and called for me to help them change it. Help them! Two of them there were, and having trouble changing a tire. I asked where they were headed for, and they said Croom, and I said I'd be right back and give them a hand, and I came straight here. They'll be here soon, Evan. They'll ask at the tavern and find out you went there for directions to our house. You'd best go to your room."

"I'll leave the house."

"And go where? In Limerick City they say that more are coming over from Dublin, and detectives from Cork as well. Go to your room and stay quiet. They'll be on us in five minutes, but if you're in your room they'll never find you."

I grabbed up my letters and snatched up the sweater I had been wearing. I opened the panel, scurried up the rope ladder, and drew it up after me. Tom raised the panel and locked it from below.

Perhaps it was only five minutes that I crouched in the darkness by the side of the trapdoor. It seemed far longer. I heard the car drive up and then the knocking at the door. I caught snatches of conversation as the two policemen searched the little cottage. Then they were on the stairs, and I could hear the conversation more clearly. Nora was insisting that they were hiding no one, no one at all.

"You bloody I.R.A.," one of the police said. "Don't you know the war's over?"

"It's not yet begun," Tom said recklessly.

The other garda was tapping at the ceiling. "I stayed in a house just like this one," he was saying. "Oh, it was years ago, when I was on the run myself. Stayed in half the houses in County Limerick and a third in County Clare. What's the name here? Dolan?"

"It is."

"Why, this is one I stayed in," the garda said. "A hiding place in the ceiling, if I remember it. What's this? Do you hear how hollow it sounds? He's up there, I swear it."

"And that's your gratitude," Nora said. "That Dolan's

house saved your life once—and may we be forgiven for it—only so that you can betray the house, yourself."

The garda was evidently working the catch to the panel. I had secured the hook on the inside, and although he opened it, the panel would not drop loose.

"That was years ago," I heard him say.

"Gratitude has a short memory, does it?"

"Years and years ago. And why keep old hatreds alive?" He'd loosened the panel slightly, enough so that his fingers could almost get a purchase on it. He tugged at it, and I felt the hook straining. It was old wood. I didn't know if it would hold.

"We're a republic now," the other garda said. "Free and independent."

"A free and independent republic under the bloody heel of the bloody English Parliament." This last from Tom.

"Oh, say it at a meeting. At a parade."

The garda had a better grip on the panel now. The hook-and-eye attachment couldn't take the strain. It was starting to pull loose.

"You're wasting your time," Nora said desperately.

"Oh, are we?"

"He was here, I'll not deny it, but he left this morning."

"And contrived to fasten the hook up there after himself, did he? I hope you don't expect an honest Irish policeman to be taken in by a snare like that, child."

"And did I ever meet one?"

"Meet what?"

"An honest Irish policeman—"

At that unfortunate moment the hook pulled out from the wood, and the panel swung open all the way, the garda following it and falling to the floor with the sudden momentum. The other reached upward, caught hold of an end of the rope ladder and pulled it free. I was in darkness at the side of the opening. I could see down, but they apparently did not see me.

The policeman who had forced the panel was getting unsteadily to his feet. The other turned to him and drew a revolver from his holster. "Wait here," he said. "I'll go in there after him."

"Take care, Liam. He's a cool one."

"No worry."

I thought suddenly of the men's toilet at Shannon Airport. I watched, silent, frozen, as the garda climbed purposefully up the rope ladder. He used one hand to steady himself and held the gun in the other. His eyes evidently didn't accustom themselves to the dark very quickly, for he looked straight at me without seeing me. A Vitamin A deficiency, perhaps.

I glanced downward. The other garda stood at the bottom of the ladder, gazing upward blindly. Tom was on his left, Nora a few feet away on the right, her jaw slack and her hands clutched together in despair. I glanced again at the climbing garda. He had reached the top now. He straightened up in the low-ceilinged room, and he roared as his head struck the beam overhead.

I took him by the shoulders and shoved. He bounced across the room, and I threw myself through the opening in the floor, like a paratrooper leaping from a plane. Between my feet, as I fell, I saw the upraised uncomprehending face of the other garda.

"Up the Republic!" someone was shouting. It was days later when I realized that it was my voice I had heard.

Chapter 8

It was neither as easy nor as glorious as the assault upon Mustafa, but it had its points. The garda dodged to one side at the last possible moment. Otherwise my feet would have landed on his shoulders, and he would have fallen like a felled steer. Instead, I hit him going away, caromed into the side of him, and he and I went sprawling in opposite directions. I scrambled to my feet and rushed at him. He was clawing at his revolver, but he had buttoned the holster and couldn't open it. He had white hair and child-blue eyes. I swung at him and missed. He lunged toward me, and Tom kicked him in the stomach just as Nora brought her shoe down on the base of his skull. That did it; he went down and out.

I barely remembered the trapdoor in time. I rushed to it, threw the rope ladder upward and saw the end of it strike the upstairs garda hard enough to put him off stride. I swung the panel back into place. He got his balance and lunged for it, and his fingers got in the way. He roared as the panel snapped on them. I opened it, and he drew out his fingers, howling like a gelded camel, and I closed the panel again and held it while Tom fastened the catch in place.

"It won't hold him," Nora said.

"I know."

"If he jumps on it—"

"I know."

But he wasn't jumping on it. Not yet. The prostrate policeman was starting to stir, and the one in the attic room was kicking at the panel. Sooner or later he would leap on it with both feet and come through on top of us. I raced down the stairs and out the door. Their car, a gray Vauxhall sedan with a siren mounted on the front fender, was in front of the cottage. They had left the keys in the ignition, reasoning, perhaps, that no one would be such a damned fool as to steal a police car.

I wrenched open the door, hopped behind where the wheel should have been. It was the wrong side, of course. I got behind the wheel and turned the ignition key, and the car coughed and stalled. I tried again, and the motor caught. I fumbled for the hand brake, released it, shifted into first, and pulled away from the curb.

There's no spare tire, I thought idiotically. They had that damned flat, so there's no spare tire, and this is dangerous—

It was definitely dangerous. I heard a gunshot and saw the white-haired cop firing at me from the second-floor window. Evidently he had recovered. Evidently he had remembered how to unbutton his holster and get at his gun. And the other one had jumped through the trap-door after all, because he was coming out the doorway toward me.

I put the accelerator pedal on the floor and went away.

The car was even worse than the bicycle had been. It had been months since I'd driven any sort of car, and I'd never driven one with right-hand drive. The Vauxhall kept drifting over to the wrong side of the road, moving into the lane of oncoming traffic as if with a will of its own. The road curved incessantly, and I continually found myself coming around a curve to encounter a Volkswagen or Triumph approaching me on the right, at which point I automatically pulled to the right and charged the little car, making for it like a bull for a muleta. I generally swung back to the left in time, but once I forced a VW off the road and no doubt scared the driver half to death.

To make matters worse, I had no particular idea where I was going until a road sign indicated I was headed for a town called Rath Luirc. I had never heard of it and didn't know whether it lay north, south, east, or west of Croom. When I reached the town and passed through it I found that the same road went on to Mallow and ultimately to Cork. This was better than returning to Limerick, but it wouldn't get me to Dublin, or to London, or to Balikesir. I was driving a stolen police car in hazardous fashion with no real destination in mind, and somehow this struck me as a distinctly imperfect way to proceed.

A few miles past Mallow I took a dirt road to the right, drove for a mile or so, and pulled off to the side of the road. The dirt road saved me the need of keeping the car on the left side, as the entire road was only a car's width wide. If I'd met anyone headed in the opposite direction, things might have become difficult, but this didn't happen. The road looked as though it didn't get much use.

I got out of the car. A trio of black-faced sheep, their sides daubed with blue paint, wandered over to the heaped-stone fence and regarded me with interest. I walked around the car and got back inside. There was a road map of Ireland in the glove compartment. I opened it and found out approximately where I was. I was approximately lost.

I put the map aside and sorted through the remaining treasures in the glove box. Three sweepstake tickets, a flashlight, a 4*d*. postage stamp with the head of Daniel O'Connell, a small chrome-plated flask of whiskey, a pair of handcuffs sans key, a St. Christopher medal on a gold-plated chain, and half of a ham sandwich neatly wrapped in wax paper. I ate the sandwich, drunk a bit of the whiskey, put the flashlight in one pocket and the flask in the other, and fastened the St. Christopher medal around my neck; I was one traveler who would need all the help he could get.

The rest I left in the car. I would have liked to take the handcuffs, feeling that I might be likely to have a use for them sooner or later, but they couldn't be used without a key. I checked the Vauxhall's trunk before I left and found only a flat tire, a bumper jack, tire iron, and a lug wrench. I could not foresee a use for any of these and left them all behind. I rolled down the windows and left the key in the ignition, a procedure which, in New York, would have guaranteed the imminent disappearance of the car. But I couldn't be sure this would happen in rural Ireland. One could not count on turning up juvenile delinquents on unpaved one-lane roads. At the least, I could hope that no one took the road for a few hours so that the car would remain undiscovered that long.

I walked back to the main road. My silk road had also been headed toward Cork, with a branch cutting off toward Killarney and points west. Thus, whoever found the car might conclude that I was headed in that direction, had car trouble, and continued toward either Cork or Killarney on foot. I didn't know how well this would throw them off the trail or for how long, but it was something. For my part, I started walking toward Mallow. I'd gone less than a mile when a car stopped, and a youngish priest gave me a lift the rest of the way.

All he wanted to talk about was the American spy. He hadn't heard about my escape in Croom, but he'd heard a strong rumor that I was in Dublin plotting to dynamite de Valera's mansion. I passed myself off as a Scot from Edinburgh spending a few months learning the Gaelic tongue in County Mayo and now touring the Irish countryside. He wasn't sufficiently interested in me to pursue the matter far enough to find the holes in my story.

I mailed about half of my letters in Mallow. A copy of the Cork *Examiner* had my picture on the front page. I pulled my cap farther down on my forehead and hurried to the bus station. There was a bus leaving for Dublin in a little over an hour, the ticket clerk told me. I had enough Irish money for a ticket and bought one. There was a darkened pub across the street. I had a plate of fried whiting and chips and drank a glass of Guinness and kept my face in the paper until it was time to catch my bus. Boarding it, presenting my ticket, walking all the way through the bus to the very back, I felt as conspicuous as if I had no clothes on. No one seemed to notice me. I'd bought a batch of paperbacks at the bus station and I read them one after another, keeping my face hidden as much as possible all the way.

We stopped for dinner in Kilkenny, then went on to Dublin through Carlow and Kildare and Naas. By sunset it had begun raining again. It was almost nine o'clock when the bus reached the terminal in Dublin. The whole trip was only 150 miles or so, but we'd had many stops and several waits. I left the bus and found the terminal crawling with gardai. Several of them looked right at me without recognizing me.

In the men's room I had a drink of whiskey from the flask, then capped it and put it back in my jacket pocket. My pockets were bulging with the flask and the flashlight. I slipped out of the terminal through a rear exit. I walked in the rain through a maze of narrow streets, not sure where I was or where I ought to be going. When I came to O'Connell Street, the main street of downtown Dublin, I felt as though I must be going in the right direction. And then I remembered that hunted men always headed for the largest cities and sought out the downtown sections of those cities with all the instinct for self-preservation of moths seeking a flame—the police always looked for hunted men in the busy downtown sections of big cities.

A pair of James Bond movies were playing in a theater a few doors down from the remains of the Nelson monument. The I.R.A. had dynamited the top of the monument a few months earlier, and the city had blown up the rest of it but hadn't yet put anything in its place. A tall man with glasses and a black attaché case was looking at the monument, then glanced at me, then looked at the monument again. I went into the cinema and sat in the back row for two and a half hours, hoping that Sean Connery could give me some sort of clue as to what I might do next. I had a pocketful of American money that I didn't dare spend, a handful of English and Irish pounds, a flashlight, a flask of whiskey (which I emptied and discarded in the course of the second film), and a St. Christopher medal. I did not have a passport, or a way of getting out of Ireland, or the slightest notion of what to do next.

James Bond was no help. Near the end of the second picture, just as Bond was heaving the girl into the pot of molten lead, I saw a man walking slowly and purposefully up and down the aisle, as if looking for an empty seat. But the theater was half empty. I looked at him again and saw that he was the same man who had looked alternately at the Nelson monument and at me. There was something familiar about him. I had the feeling I'd seen him before at the bus station.

I sank down into my seat and lowered my head. He made another grand tour of the cinema, walking to the front and back again, his eyes passing over me with no flicker of recognition. I couldn't breathe. I waited for him to see me, and then he walked on and out of the theater while I struggled for breath and wiped cold perspiration from my forehead.

But he was there when I came out. I knew he would be.

I tried to melt into the shadows and slip away to the left, and at first I thought I had lost him. When I looked over my shoulder, he was still there. I walked very slowly to the corner, turned it, and took off at a dead run. I ran straight for two blocks while people stared at me as if I had gone mad, then turned another corner and slowed down again. A cab came by. I hailed it, and it stopped for me.

"Just drive," I said.

"Where, sir?"

I couldn't think of the answer to that. "A pub," I managed to say. "Someplace where I can get a good dinner."

The cab still had not moved. "There's a fine restaurant just across the street, sir. And quite reasonable, as well."

My man came around the corner. He didn't have his attaché case now, I noticed. I tried to hide myself, but he saw me.

I said, "I had a row with my wife. I think she's following me. Drive around the block a few times and then drop me off at that restaurant, can you?"

He could and did. My pursuer had stepped to the curb now and was trying to hail a cab of his own. My driver charged forward as the light turned. I watched out of the back window. The man had still not caught a cab. My driver turned a corner, drove for a few blocks, then turned another corner. I settled back in the seat and relaxed.

I kept checking the back window. Now and then I saw a cab behind us and had the driver turn corners until we lost it. Finally he told me no one could possibly have followed us. "I'll take you to that restaurant now, sir. You'll have a good meal there."

He dropped me in front of the restaurant. As I opened the door I glanced over my shoulder and saw the tall man with glasses. He was still trying to catch a cab. He saw me, and our eyes met, and I felt dizzy. I pushed open the door of the restaurant and went inside. When I looked back, I saw him crossing the street after me.

The headwaiter showed me to a table. I ordered a brandy and sat facing the door. I had never before felt so utterly stupid. I had escaped and then, brainlessly, I had returned to precisely the place where the tall man was waiting.

The door opened. The tall man came in, looked my way, then glanced out the door again. His face clouded for a moment and he seemed to hesitate. Perhaps, I thought, he was afraid to attempt to capture me by himself. No doubt I was presumed armed and dangerous.

Could I make a break for it? Surprise had worked twice before, with Mustafa and the two gardai. But I couldn't avoid the feeling that the third time might be the charm. This man was prepared. He was walking toward my table—

Still, it seemed worth a try. I looked past him as though I did not see him, my hands gripping the table from below. When he was close enough I would heave it at him, then run.

Then over his shoulder I saw the gardai—three of them, in uniform—coming through the doorway. If I got past him, I would only succeed in running into their arms. It was as though I were drowning. All at once my official misdeeds of the past two days rushed through my mind: assaulting a Turk, entering Ireland illegally, traveling with false papers, bicycle theft, assault and battery of two Irish policemen, auto theft, auto abandonment, resisting arrest—

The tall man with the glasses stumbled, fell forward toward me. His right hand broke his fall, his left brushed against my right side. He said, "Mooney's, Talbot Street," then got to his feet and swept past me.

And the gardai, solemn as priests, walked on by my table and surrounded him. One took his right arm, the other his left, and the third marched behind with a drawn pistol. They marched him out of the restaurant and left me there alone.

I could only stare after them, I and all the other patrons of the restaurant. It was late, and most of the other diners were about half-lit. At the doorway the tall man made his move. He kicked backward at the garda with the pistol, wrenched himself free from the grasp of the other two, and broke into a run.

Along with other diners, I pressed forward. I heard two short blasts on a police whistle, then a brace of gunshots. I reached the door and saw the tall man rushing across the street. A garda was shooting at him. The tall man spun around, gun in hand, and began firing wildly. A bullet shattered the restaurant window, and I dropped to the floor. A fresh fusillade of shots rang out. I peered over the window ledge and saw the tall man lying in a heap in the middle of the street. There were sirens wailing in the distance. One of the gardai had taken a bullet through one hand and was bleeding fiercely.

And no one was paying any attention to me.

I went back to my table. My hands were trembling. I couldn't control them. I thought for a moment that I must have gone schizophrenic, that it was I who attempted to escape the police and who was shot down by them, and that it was a symptom of my madness that I thought it had happened to someone else. The waiter brought my brandy. I drank it straight down and ordered another.

Mooney's, Talbot Street, he had said. I didn't know what he meant, or who he was, or who he thought me to be. Why had he followed me? If the police were following him, why should he follow me? What was Mooney's? Was I supposed to meet him there? It seemed unlikely that he would ever keep the appointment.

Then I found in my right coat pocket, where he must have placed it when he fell, a metal brass-colored disc perhaps an inch and a half across. Stamped upon it were the numerals 249.

At that point it was easy enough to figure out the what, if not the why. I worked my way back to O'Connell Street and found Talbot Street, just around the corner from the cinema. Mooney's was a crowded pub halfway down the block. I found the checkroom and presented the brass disc. As I had expected, the attendant handed over the black attaché case, and I left a shilling on the saucer. I closed myself in a cubicle in the men's room and propped the attaché case upon my lap. It was not locked. I opened it.

On top was an envelope with my name on it. I drew a single sheet of hotel stationery from it. The message was in pencil, written in a hurried scrawl:

Tanner—
I just hope you're who I think you are. Deliver the goods to the right people and they'll take care of you. The passports are clean. Big trouble for everybody if delivery isn't made.

Six hours later I was in Madrid.

Chapter 9

Esteban Robles lived on Calle de la Sangre—Blood Street—a dim, narrow two-block lane in the student quarter south of the university. The morning was hot, the sun blindingly bright, the sky a perfect cloudless blue. I abandoned my heavy jacket at the airport and changed some British pounds for pesetas at the Iberian Airways desk.

My cab driver had some difficulty finding Calle de la Sangre. He tore furiously up and down the narrow streets of the quarter and chatted about the weather and the bulls and Vietnam. My Spanish was South American, and I told him I was from Venezuela. We then discussed the menace of Fidel. He wanted to know if it was true that the Fidelistas gelded priests and ravished nuns. The thought infused him with scandalized lust.

I found Robles on the third floor of a drab tenement permeated with cooking smells. His room resembled the cell of a slovenly monk—a desk piled high with books and newspaper clippings and cigarette stubs, another heap of books in a corner, four empty wine bottles, a pan of leftover beans and rice, and a narrow cot that sagged in the middle. The floor was incompletely covered with linoleum, its pattern obscured by years of dirt. Robles himself was a young fellow with the body of a matador and the bearded face of a protest marcher. I knew him as a fellow member of the Federation of Iberian Anarchists. It was a dangerous thing to be in Spain, and I had trouble convincing him that I was not an agent of the Civil Guard.

Perhaps I shouldn't have bothered. If he had gone on thinking of me as an agent of Franco's secret police, he would have cooperated with me. Instead, I went to great lengths to convince him who I was and I only succeeded in terrifying him. He kept darting stricken looks at the door of his room, as if men with drawn sabers might burst in at any moment and lead us both off to prison.

"But what do you want here?" he kept demanding. "But why do you come to me?"

"I have to go to Turkey," I explained.

"Am I an airplane? This is not safe. You must go."

"I need your help."

"My help?" He glanced again at the door. "I cannot help you. The police are everywhere. And I have nowhere for you to stay. Nowhere. One small bed is all I own, and I sleep in it myself. You cannot stay here."

"I want to get out of Spain."

"So do I. So does everyone. I could make a grand fortune in America. I could become a hairdresser. Jackie Kennedy."

"Pardon me?"

"I would set her hair and make a fortune."

"I don't think I—"

"Instead, I rot in Madrid." He fingered his beard. "I could set Jackie Kennedy's hair and make a fortune. Lady Bird Johnson. Are you a hairdresser?"

"No."

"I have had no breakfast. There is a café downstairs,

but you cannot go. They will shoot you in the street like
a dog. Can you speak Spanish?"

We had been speaking Spanish all along. I was beginning to suspect that Robles was mad.

"There is a café," he said. "They know me there. So
they will not give me credit." He glanced at the door
again. His fear was so genuine that I was beginning to
share it. At any moment the Civil Guard would come in
and shoot us down like hairdressers.

"I have no money," he said.

I gave him some Spanish money and told him to get
breakfast for both of us. He snatched the notes from
me, glanced again at the door, lit a cigarette, smoked
furiously, dropped ashes on the floor, then threw himself on the cot.

"If I order breakfast for two," he said, "they will
know I have someone up here."

"Tell them you have a girl."

"Here? In this goat pen?"

"Well—"

"They know me," he said sorrowfully. "They know
I never have a girl. You should never have come here.
Why did you leave America? Mamie Eisenhower. Who
sets her hair?"

"I don't know."

"You create trouble. How can we eat? No one will
believe you are a girl. Your hair is too short."

I suggested that he eat breakfast at the café and buy
food for me. He leaped from the bed and threw his
arms around me. "You are a genius," he shouted. "You
will save us all."

When he went out, I tried to lock the door. The lock
was broken. I sat on his bed and read a poor Spanish
translation of Kropotkin's essay on "Mutual Aid." He

had evidently read it over many times as the text was extensively underlined, but the underlining made no sense at all. He underlined trivia—unimportant adjectives, place names, that sort of thing.

He came back with some sweet rolls and a cardboard container of *café con leche*. While I ate he told me of his breakfast—four eggs, slices of fried ham, fresh juice, a dish of saffron rice with peas and peppers. I listened to all this while I ate my rolls and sipped the bad coffee.

"I will get another bed," he said. "Or, if that is not possible, you may sleep upon the floor. My house is your house."

"I won't be staying that long."

"But you must stay! It is not safe in the streets. They would shoot you like a dog." He smiled engagingly. "You will stay," he said, "as long as you have money."

"Oh."

"Have you much money?"

"Very little."

He looked at the door again. "On the other hand," he said, "you would perhaps be uncomfortable upon the floor. And it is not safe here. Every day the police come and beat me. Do you believe me?"

"Yes."

"You do? You should have stayed in America. What do you want from me?"

"A few hours of solitude. I want the use of your room for several hours and then I want you to take me to someone who can help me get out of Spain."

"You will go to Portugal?"

"No. To France."

"Ah. Now you want me to leave?"

"Yes."

"Why?"

"I want to sleep."

"In my bed?"

"Yes."

"It is not sanitary."

I took some more Spanish money from my wallet. "You could pass a few hours in the cinema," I suggested.

He was gone like a shot. I closed the door and wished that it had a functioning lock on it. I went to the window and drew the shade. It was badly torn. Through the hole in the shade I looked into a room in the building next door. A rather plump girl with long black hair was dressing. I watched her for a few moments, then left the window and sat on Esteban's bed and opened my black attaché case. A gift of Providence, I thought. An ideal survival kit for a hunted man. It had everything I might need—money, passports, and documents so secret I had no idea what they were.

Along with the unsigned and unintelligible note, the attaché case had contained a heavy cardigan sweater with a London label, a change of underwear, a pair of dreadful Argyle socks, a safety razor with no blades, a toothbrush, a can of tooth powder made in Liverpool, and a Japanese rayon tie with a fake Countess Mara crest. There was also a Manila envelope holding banded packages of British, American, and Swiss currency—two hundred pounds, one hundred fifty dollars, and just over two thousand Swiss francs. Another larger envelope contained three passports. The American passport was in the name of William Alan Traynor, the British in the name of R. Kenneth Leyden, and the Swiss for Henri Boehm. Each showed a rather poor photograph of the tall man. On the American passport he was wearing glasses. On the other two he was not.

A third Manila envelope, carefully sealed with heavy tape, held the mysterious documents. These, evidently, were the "goods" that I was to deliver to "the right people." I had attempted to slit the tape with my thumbnail in the manner of James Bond opening a packet of cigarettes. This proved impossible, so I had laboriously peeled off the tape in the privacy of the Dublin lavatory and had a look at the contents of the parcel. It had made no particular sense to me then; now, in the equally dismal atmosphere of Esteban Robles' dirty little room, it remained as impenetrable as ever.

Half a dozen sheets of photocopied blueprints. Blueprints for what? I had no idea. A dozen sheets of ruled notebook paper covered with either the mental doodling of a mathematician or some esoteric code. A batch of carefully drawn diagrams. A whole packet of confidential information, no doubt stolen from someone and destined for someone else. But stolen from whom? And destined for whom? And indicating what?

When I first opened the case it had scarcely mattered. I had packed everything away and taken a taxi to the Dublin airport. There were no flights to the Continent until morning, I learned, unless I wanted to fly first to London and then make connections to Paris. I did not want to go to London at all, not now. I used the American passport to buy a ticket to Madrid and paid for it with American money. I left the case in a locker and went back into town. At the lost and found counter of the bus station I explained that I'd left a pair of glasses on a bus, and asked whether anyone had turned them in. Five pairs were brought to me, and I would have liked to try them on until I found a pair that wasn't too hard on my eyes, but this might have aroused suspicion. I picked a pair that looked rather like the ones in William Alan Traynor's passport photograph and thanked the clerk and left.

By flight time I was back at the airport. I took my attaché case from the locker, lodged the envelope of unidentifiable secret papers between my shirt and my skin, and incorporated the currency with my own small fund of money. I tucked my two extra passports (and Mustafa Ibn Ali's) into a pocket, combed my hair to conform to the passport photo, and put on the glasses. Their previous owner had evidently combined extreme myopia with severe astigmatism. I hadn't worn them five minutes before I had a blinding headache.

I'd have preferred using another passport and going without glasses, but there were good reasons for being Traynor. The glasses did change my appearance somewhat, and with my own photo plastered over every newspaper in Ireland it seemed worthwhile to avoid being recognized as Evan Michael Tanner. Besides that, the Traynor passport was the only one with an Irish entry visa stamped on it. The tall man had evidently used it to enter Ireland six weeks earlier.

I got blindly through customs, with my attaché case receiving only a cursory check. The flight to Madrid was happily uneventful, the landing smooth enough. The Aer Lingus stewardess made cheerful announcements in English and Irish and served reasonably good coffee. I kept my glasses on and kept my eyes closed behind them. Whenever I looked at anything, it blurred before my eyes, and my head ached all over again.

Once I was through Spanish customs, I dug out the R. Kenneth Leyden passport and showed it as identification when I changed pounds to pesetas at the Iberia desk. I put the glasses away, hoping I would never have to wear them again, and headed for the one man in Madrid who could help me on my way to Balikesir.

At the time, never having met Esteban Robles, I had had no idea he was a lunatic.

The packet of secret papers bothered me. If I had known just what they were, I might have had some idea what to do with them. Knowing neither their source nor their destination nor their nature, I was wholly in the dark.

I could destroy them, of course, but that might prove to be a bad idea if they were as valuable as they seemed to be. I could mail them anonymously to the Irish Government—the Irish certainly seemed anxious to recover them. I could send them to the American Consulate, thereby doing what could only be regarded as patriotic while passing the buck neatly enough.

And yet, in a sense, I felt a sort of debt to my anonymous benefactor, the tall man who had been shot down by the Irish police. However invalid his assumptions of my identity, however suspect his motives, he had done me a good turn. He had provided me with three passports to spirit me out of Ireland and away from the manhunt that sooner or later would have caught up with me. He had endowed me with a supply of capital that would help me on my way to Balikesir. My own funds were perilously close to being depleted, and his pounds and dollars and francs were welcome.

He had also supplied me with a change of underclothing and socks, which I now put on. It is difficult, if not impossible, to wear the socks and underwear of a dead man without feeling somehow obliged to carry out his mission. But who was he? And which side was he on?

He was not on the Irish side; that much was obvious. All right, then, suppose he was an enemy of Ireland. Why would he be spying on Ireland? What precious information could the Irish possibly have that he or his employers would want? And who could his employers be? The British? The Russians? The CIA? The answer was unattainable without a knowledge of the nature of the documents, and they remained as impenetrable as ever.

At least no one knew I had them. I could destroy them or retain them or send them somewhere and, for better or for worse, I would be forever out of it. Unless—

It was a horrible thought.

It was possible, I thought suddenly, that the tall man had let someone know what he'd done with the documents. He could have sent off a wire or dashed off a fast letter to his employers. *They're on to me but I'm sending the stuff with your man Tanner,* he might have wired.

And someone at the other end would have realized that Tanner was not their man at all, and that he ought to be gotten hold of in a hurry. And then what?

Things, I thought, were getting awfully damned involved.

I looked at my three passports. If the tall man had spread the word, those passports were dangerous. His men would probably know the names he was using— Traynor and Leyden and Boehm. If he was a Yugoslavian spy, for example, it would not do to present any of the three passports at the Yugoslavian border. But this left me as much in the dark as ever. If I only knew for whom he worked, I could avoid those countries. But I didn't. Maybe he was a *Spanish* spy, as far as that went—though why Spain would be spying on Ireland I could not imagine.

I was getting nowhere. I gave it up, put everything back in the attaché case, closed it, and stretched out on Esteban's unsanitary bed. My head was spinning, my stomach recoiling from the combined effect of fear and bad coffee. I went through my little repertoire of Yoga exercises, relaxing, breathing deeply, and generally easing myself out of my blue funk.

Esteban had still not returned when I got up from the bed. I tucked my attaché case under the bed and left the room. In a bookstore near the university I bought a pocket atlas and calculated a route to the French border. I stopped at a café and had a glass of bitter red wine. I thumbed through the atlas again and plotted the remainder of my trip. Spain, France, Italy, Yugoslavia, and Turkey—that seemed the best route. That gave me four borders to cross, with each one promising to be slightly more hazardous than the one before it. But it could be done. I was certain it could be done.

Esteban was waiting for me. He ran to me and embraced me furiously. "You were gone," he said accusingly. "When I came back, you were gone."

"I went out for some air."

"Ah, who can breathe in the fetid stench of fascism? But the streets are dangerous. You should not have gone out. I feared that something might have happened to you."

"Nothing did."

"Ah." He scratched at his beard. "It is not safe for you here. It is not safe for either of us. We must leave."

"We?"

"Both of us!" He spread his arms wide as if to embrace the beauty of the idea. "We will go to France. This afternoon we rush to the border. Tonight, under the cloak of darkness, we slip across the border like sardines. Who will see us?"

"Who?"

"No one!" He clapped his hands. "I know the way, my friend. One goes to the border, one talks to the right people, and like that"—he snapped his fingers soundlessly—"it is arranged. In no time at all we are across the border and into France. I will go to Paris. Can you imagine me in Paris? I shall become the most famous hairdresser in all of Paris."

"Are you a hairdresser in Madrid?"

He frowned at me. "One cannot be a hairdresser in Madrid. Would Jackie Kennedy come to Madrid to have her hair set? Or Christine Keeler? Or Nina Khrushchev? Or—"

"Have you ever been to France?"

"Never!"

"Have you been to the border?"

"Never in my life!"

"But you know people there?"

"Not a soul!" He could not contain himself and rushed to embrace me again. His body odor was almost identical to that of Mustafa.

"I don't know," I said. "I'm not sure it sounds like the best of all possible plans. It might be dangerous for us to travel together."

"Dangerous? It would be dangerous for us to separate."

"Why?"

"Why?" He spread his hands. "Why not?"

"Esteban—"

He turned from me and walked to the window. "She is not there now," he said. "There is a girl across the way, very fat. Sometimes one can see her."

"I know."

"Sometimes she has a man there, and I watch them together. Not always the same man, either. I was going to watch her tonight. It is sad, is it not? Tonight I will be in France and I will never be able to watch the fat girl again. Do you think she is a whore?"

"No. Maybe. I don't know. What does it—"

"Perhaps she would come to France with us. I will set her hair and she will become famous."

I reached under the bed for my attaché case. I wanted only to escape this madman. The case was not there.

"Esteban—"

"You look for this?" He handed it to me. I opened it and checked its contents. Everything seemed to be there.

"You see," he said solemnly, "it would be very dangerous for us to be separated. Every day at four o'clock the Guardia Civil comes to check on me. They do not beat me—that was something I made up for you—but they come every day to make sure I am still here. I am subversive."

"I believe it."

"But they do not feel that I am dangerous. Do you understand? They only check to see who it is whom I have been seeing and what correspondence I have received and matters of that sort. I always tell them everything. That is the only way to deal with these fascist swine. One must tell them everything, everything. Only then can they be sure that I'm not dangerous."

If they thought the foul little lunatic was not dangerous, then they did not know him as well as I did.

"So if they come today, I must tell them about you. The names on your three passports, and the papers with the letters and numbers upon them, and—"

"No."

"But what else can I do, my friend? You see why we must go to France together? If we are separated, the police will know all about you. But if we are together, then you are safe. And under the protective cloak of darkness we will steal across the border into France, and I will become famous. We are like brothers, you and I. Closer than brothers. Like twins who shared the same womb. Do you comprehend?"

I was taller than Esteban, and heavier. I thought of knocking him down and fleeing, but I had done that too often lately. It couldn't work forever. Sooner or later one would run out of beginner's luck. And, if there was any truth in that old chestnut about a madman's possessing superhuman strength, Esteban would be able to wipe the floor with me.

"When will the Guard visit you?"

"In a few hours. So you see that it is good you came to me. In all of Madrid it was to Esteban Robles that you came. Is it not fate?"

In all of Madrid, it was to Esteban Robles that I came. Of all my little band of conspirators, of all my troupe of subversives and schemers and plotters, I had sought out the Judas goat of the secret police. And now I had to take the madman with me to France.

"If you want to go to France, why don't you just go?"

"I have no money, my brother."

"If I gave you money—"

"And I am not clever. I am an artist, a grand artist, but I am not clever. Do I know anything about crossing borders? About stealing through the pass under the protective cloak of night? I know nothing. But with you to guide me and to bribe the proper persons—"

"I could give you money."

"But we *need* each other, my friend!"

Perhaps, I told myself, he might prove useful. At least he spoke Spanish like a native, a natural enough accomplishment for a Spaniard, but one that might be of use. No, I decided, he would *not* prove useful. He would be a nuisance and a danger, but I had to take him along. I was stuck with the lunatic.

"We will go?"

"Yes," I said.

"Now?"

"Now."

He went to the window. "She is still not in her room. Shall we wait for her? The fat little whore would probably be happy to accompany us to Paris."

"No."

"No?"

"No."

"You do not like fat girls? For my part—"

"We go together," I said. "Just the two of us, Esteban. You and I. No one else."

His eyes were unutterably sad. "I never have a girl," he said. "Never, never, never. The one time I found a girl who would go with me, I was fooled. You know how I mean? I thought it was this pretty American girl, but when we got back to my room, it turned out to be a *marica* from New York. A fairy. It was better than nothing, but when one has one's heart set on a girl—you are sure you do not want the fat little—"

"There will be girls in Paris, Esteban."

"Ah! You are my brother. You are more than my brother. You are—"

Words failed him, and I was again suffocated in his embrace.

Chapter 10

Before we went anywhere, I took Esteban to a barber and had him shaved. He fought the idea every step of the way, but I managed to convince him that Frenchmen did not wear beards. Without it he looked less like a fiery anarchist and more like a backward child. I had the barber give him a haircut while he was at it and had my own hair cut so that it looked a little more like the passport photos and a little less like the picture of Evan Tanner that the newspapers had printed. Then, with Esteban in one hand and the attaché case in another, I left Madrid.

We took a train as far as Zaragoza, a bus east to Lérida and another bus north to Sort, a small village a little over twenty miles from the frontier. In Zaragoza I left Esteban for a few moments at a restaurant while I visited a few shops and spent a few pesetas. He was still eating when I returned. He slept on the bus ride. The bus to Sort was not heated, and the last lap of our journey was cold, with the sun down and the wind blowing through the drafty bus. I gave the tall man's sweater to Esteban, who promptly went back to sleep. I wished that I had kept my Irish jacket or had brought along a flask of brandy.

At Sort I poked Esteban awake and led him off the bus. He lit a cigarette and blew smoke in my face. He had been doing this all the way from Madrid, and it was beginning to annoy me.

"Are we in France?"

"No."

"Where are we?"

"Some place called Sort."

"In Spain?"

"Yes."

"I have never heard of it."

There were four cafés in the town. We visited each of them and drank brandy. The third of the four turned out to be the worst, so we returned to it. Esteban appeared to be about half-lit. Among his many other talents, he was evidently incapable of holding liquor.

We sat in a dingy back booth. He began talking in a loud voice about the joys of Paris and the need to escape from the reeking stench of fascism. I had two choices—I could try to sober him up or I could get him drunk enough to pass out. I had the waitress bring a full bottle of brandy and I poured one shot after another into Esteban, and ultimately his head rolled and his eyes closed and he sagged in his chair and quietly passed out.

I stood up and walked to the bar. A large man with sad eyes and a drooping moustache stood beside me. "Your friend," he said, "says things which one should not say in the presence of strangers."

"My friend is sick," I said.

"Ah."

"My friend has a sickness in his mind and must go for treatment. He must go to the hospital."

"There is no hospital in Sort."

"We cannot stay in Sort, then, for I must take him to a hospital."

"There is a hospital in Barcelona. A fine modern hospital, where your friend would be most comfortable."

"We cannot go to the hospital in Barcelona. There is only one hospital that will care for my friend properly."

"In Madrid, then?"

"In Paris."

"In Paris," he said. I poured us each a brandy. He thanked me and said that I was a gentleman, and I said that it was pleasant to drink in the company of worldly men like himself.

"It is far," he said slowly, "to Paris."

"It is."

"And one must have the right papers to cross the frontier."

"My friend has no papers."

"He will have difficulty."

"It is true," I said. "He will have great difficulty."

"It will be impossible for him."

"For worldly men," I said carefully, "for worldly men of goodwill, men who understand one another and understand how life is to be lived, I have heard it said that nothing is impossible."

"There is truth in what you say."

"It is as I have heard it said by wiser men than I."

"It is a wise man who listens to and remembers the words of other wise men."

"You do me much honor, señor."

"You honor me to drink with me, señor."

We had another brandy each. He motioned me to follow him, and we sat at the table next to Esteban. He was still asleep.

"Call me Manuel," the man said. "And I shall call you what?"

"Enrique."

"It is my pleasure to know you, Enrique."

"The pleasure is my pleasure."

"Perhaps among my acquaintances there are men who could help you and your unfortunate friend. When one lives in a town for all of one's life, one knows a great many people."

"I would greatly appreciate your help."

"You will wait here?"

"I will," I said.

He stopped at the bar and said something to the bartender. Then he disappeared into the night. I ordered a cup of black coffee and poured a little brandy into it. When Esteban opened his eyes, I made him drink more of the brandy. He passed out again.

Manuel returned while I was still sipping my coffee. Two other men accompanied him. They stood in the bar and talked in a language I did not understand. I believe it was Basque. The Basque language is one I do not speak or understand, an almost impossible language to learn if one is not born to it. The grammatical construction is as much of a nightmare as the language of the Hopi Indians. I felt very much at a disadvantage. I am not used to being unable to understand other people's speech.

Manuel left his companions at the bar and approached our table. "I have consulted with my friends," he said. "They are of the opinion that something can be done for you."

"May God reward their kindness."

"It must be this night."

"We are ready."

He looked doubtfully at Esteban. "And is he ready, also?"

"Yes."

"Then come with me."

I had trouble getting Esteban to his feet. He swayed groggily and offered up dramatic curses to fascism and the state of the beautician's profession in Madrid. Manuel turned to his friends at the bar, touched his head with his forefinger, then pointed at Esteban and shrugged expressively. He took one of Esteban's arms, and I took the other, and we walked him out into the night.

The other two men followed us. Half a mile from the café we entered a dingy one-room hut. The smaller of Manuel's two friends, with long sideburns and denim pants frayed at the cuffs, moved around the room lighting candles. The other uncapped a flask of sweet wine and passed it around. I didn't let Esteban have any. It seemed time to sober him up a bit.

Manuel introduced us all around. The small man with the sideburns was called Pablo; the other, fat, balding, and sweaty, was Vicente. I was Enrique and Esteban was Esteban.

"I have it that you wish to go to France," Vicente said.

"Yes, and to Paris."

"I will set the hair of Brigitte Bardot," said Esteban.

"But the border is difficult."

"So I have heard."

Pablo said something quickly in Basque. Vicente answered him, then turned to me and resumed in Spanish. "You and your friend have a sympathetic reason for going to France. You must take your friend to a hospital, is it not so?"

"It is so."

"For such fine purposes, one can bend laws. But you must know, my friend, that these are dangerous times. Many smugglers attempt to take contraband over the border."

I said nothing. Manuel said something in Basque. I was furious that I had never been able to learn the language. I remembered one sentence that I had stubbornly committed to memory. *"I will meet you at the jai alai fronton."* The Basque construction for this is torture—*I the jai alai fronton at which is played the game of jai alai in the act of meeting I have you in the future.* I don't know how the Basques learn it.

"So you see," said Vicente, "that it is necessary for us to examine your possessions so that we may assure ourselves that you are not smugglers."

"I see."

"For we help willingly but only when the motives of those we help cannot be called into question."

I propped the black attaché case on a rickety card table and opened it. Pablo and Vicente gathered around, while Manuel stayed with Esteban. The various papers were passed over without a second glance. The clothes attracted no particular attention. The items I had purchased in Zaragoza received the lion's share of attention.

"Ah," said Vicente. "And what is this?"

"Beautician supplies."

Esteban came rushing over to me. "For my salon!" He embraced me. "You are my friend, my brother. What have you bought for me?"

"Your supplies, Esteban."

"My brother!"

Pablo was sorting through the bag of cheap cosmetics I had picked up. There were several plastic combs, a pair of scissors, some hair curlers, hardly the elaborate equipment one would use in a beauty parlor. He picked up a tin box of face powder, opened it, sniffed, and looked at me with raised eyebrows.

"Face powder," I said.

Vicente licked a finger, dipped it into the can of face powder, licked it again, smiled, and said something in Basque to Manuel and Pablo. They began to laugh happily.

"Perhaps you will leave this here," Vicente said.

"But it is necessary that we take it with us."

"Ah, but can you not get better face powder in Paris? The French are renowned for their cosmetics, so I have heard."

"This is special powder."

"I can see that it is."

"We have a great need for it."

"A face powder with little scent to it," Vicente said. "A face powder with a sweet taste, and yet a bitter undertaste. This is a most remarkable powder."

"My friend obtains great results with this powder."

The three of them laughed uproariously. Esteban was utterly baffled. He couldn't understand what was so important about a tin of powder or what caused men to laugh over it. I did not enlighten him.

Vicente dropped the tin of powder back into my attaché case. I closed the case, and Vicente threw a heavy arm around my shoulder. "We can help you," he said. "And I think you are wise to take the face powder with you, for it would be difficult to locate this brand in Paris, would it not?"

"Most difficult."

"For so many powders are applied with a powder puff, and this one requires a needle, does it not?"

I said nothing.

"We will take you to the border, Enrique. But we must go now."

"That is good."

"And I will carry your suitcase."

I looked at him.

"In case you are searched, señor. It is advisable."

"But in the suitcase—"

"The face powder, my friend."

We played with that one. Finally he agreed that he would carry the powder only at the moment of crossing. Pablo asked to see the tin again. I opened the case and showed it to him. He left hurriedly, explaining that he had to obtain provisions for the journey. Vicente brought out the flask of wine, and we drank to the success of our travels.

When Pablo returned, we got under way. Manuel said good-bye to us and headed back to the café. Vicente led us to a donkey cart piled high with straw. Elaborately, he explained to me how the crossing would be managed. He needn't have bothered. I had seen the scene in countless films. At the border, he told me, we would ride on the wagon with the straw covering us, while he and Pablo rode in front. Thus, he said, delighted with his own ingenuity, the border guards would think there was only a load of straw on the wagon, when actually there would be two men beneath the straw whom they would not see.

"Two men and an attaché case," I said.

"Of course," Vicente said. He looked terribly sad. "Now the arrangements of the money," he said. "We have expenses, you understand. Certain money must be passed on to certain persons. I am sure you comprehend—"

"How much?"

He quoted a price that came to less than $50 U.S. I had a feeling he would spend that much or more bribing the border guards. I started to bargain, just to avoid being too delighted with the price, and he almost instantly knocked it down a third. He wanted this fare, I realized. He wasn't about to let us walk away.

I paid him the money. It would be a long ride, he said, and no doubt we would wish to sleep. We could stretch out on top of the hay and cover ourselves with blankets and we need not get under the hay until he told us. It would be easiest to cross the frontier at the corner of Andorra, he said. We would cross two borders, first passing from Spain into Andorra, then from that tiny Basque republic into France. But that, he said, was much the easiest way. The guards were less vigorous at those posts, and they were his friends.

Esteban and I climbed onto the hay. Pablo gave us each a blanket, and we stretched out on the hay and wrapped ourselves in the blankets. The night was cooler now, the sky alive with stars. Pablo and Vicente climbed up on the little platform behind the donkey, and the animal shifted into gear and started for the border. I lay still, watching the stars, my hand coiled tightly around the grip of the attaché case.

In the darkness Esteban whispered, "But your name is not Enrique."

I told him to be still. Then, after I thought he had dropped off to sleep again, he was back with more questions. "When did you buy me those supplies? The equipment for the beauty parlor?"

"I will tell you later."

"Tell me now."

I looked over at our two escorts. I wondered if they could hear or if it would matter.

I said, "I bought them for you in Zaragoza."

"It was good of you."

"Don't mention it."

"But if I may say so, my brother, I think you were cheated."

"How?"

"The shears are cheap. They won't last. And the Cosmetics are of the poorest sort. On a shop girl one might use such inferior goods, but on the wife of Charles de Gaulle—"

"You'll set her hair?"

"And make a fortune. What is all this fuss about the face powder?"

"It is forbidden to bring face powder into France."

"But why?"

"There is a very high tariff. To protect the French manufacturers, you see."

"But to make such a fuss over one tin? And I heard the fat one say that it has no smell and tastes sweet."

"Go to sleep, Esteban."

"There are many things that I do not understand."

"Do you want to go to Paris?"

"With all my heart, friend."

"Then go to sleep."

He fell silent. His was a hurt silence at first. He wanted me to hold his hand and tell him how good it would be for him in Paris, how they would welcome him to the town, how he would set the hair of the world's most important women. He was a madman and a nuisance, yet in his own disquieting way he was good company for a trip of this sort. He gave me an unusual amount of self-confidence. He was so utterly lost, so incapable of coping with any situation, that by comparison I felt myself wholly in command of things.

The donkey moved steadily onward. Smoke from Vicente's cigar wafted back over us. The road we followed wound slowly uphill, leveling off now and then, circling in and out of the mountains, then climbing upward at a sharper inclination. I lay with my eyes closed and did my Yoga exercises from time to time, getting as much rest as I could. It was at times like this, times when one had to spend several hours doing nothing at all, that I envied those who slept. Esteban could close his eyes and lose touch with the world. He could blank out his mind to all but dreams and pass over several hours in an instant of subjective time. I had to lie there in the dark with nothing to do but wait.

This had not bothered me in years. Once I originally adjusted to going without sleep, I had always contrived to have something to do, someone to talk to, something to read or study. No matter how long one lives, awake or asleep, one can never know all that there is to know. There are, for example, several hundred languages spoken throughout the world. It would take the greater portion of a lifetime to learn them all. Alone in my apartment, stretched out on my bed listening to a stack of learn-while-you-sleep records, I could rest mind and body and add another language to my collection—and not grow bored.

Lying on a mound of hay, staring at the stars and listening to the sounds of the night and the snores of Esteban and the occasional incomprehensible chatter of Vicente and Pablo, was as bad in its own way as rotting for nine days in an Istanbul jail cell.

I thought of getting up, getting out of the wagon and running alongside the donkey for a while. Or perhaps I could sit with Pablo and Vicente and talk with them in Spanish. The donkey seemed to be moving at about six or seven miles an hour. We were twenty miles from the frontier, and with the circuitous route we were following it seemed likely that we would travel forty miles to go twenty. It would be dawn or very close to it before we reached the border, and I did not feel like lying in the straw for that long a time.

As it turned out, it was a good thing I stayed where I was.

I heard Pablo speaking Spanish. "I believe we may stop now. They have not moved or made a sound for some miles."

"You are certain?"

"Call to them. See if they answer."

Vicente called out, "Enrique? Are you asleep?"

I did not say anything. I heard Esteban shift in his sleep and wanted to hit him with something. He had to remain still now, or we were in trouble.

"They are sleeping, Vicente."

"All right."

The cart slowed, then stopped. I heard them drop down from the driver's platform and come around to the rear of the cart.

"They sleep."

"Can you be sure?"

A hand touched my foot, raised it a few inches, then let it fall. I stayed limp.

"They sleep, Vicente. It is time to take the powder. Later will be difficult."

"But he said that he would let me carry it across the border for him."

"He will think of something by then. Some trick."

"You are right. Perhaps—"

"No."

"In one instant I could slash both their throats. I would draw two red lines upon their necks, and they would be no cause for worry. And then—"

I tensed in the darkness. I saw him in my mind, knife

drawn, bending over us. I could kick out, I thought. Kick out hard and then jump backward and hope to throw myself clear. I could—

"And when their friends come? Surely you do not think that ones like this could carry something of such importance themselves. Their clothes are poor, and their shoes worn. The powder is worth a fortune."

"They are couriers, then."

"Couriers, yes. And if they do not arrive, there will be trouble, and men will come looking for them. But if they arrive without the powder, they will be in trouble themselves."

"I do not know, Pablo—"

Keep talking, Pablo. I thought. Keep talking.

"It is all the more reason why we will make the switch now," Pablo went on. "Then later we will ask to carry the powder across the border. This Enrique will argue with us. We will finally let him have his own way. Then, when he discovers the powder is gone, he will know that someone else must have taken it. That it was not we who did it."

"Where is it?"

"In the case he carries."

"Ah."

Hands fastened on the attaché case and took it gently from my loose grasp. The catch was opened. A few seconds later hands slid the case back where it had been, fastened once more.

"He will never know," said Pablo.

"And the other?"

"Nor will the other."

"The other is a madman."

"I think not," said Pablo. "I think they are very clever, these two, and that the other only pretends to be a madman. One may do well at times by pretending to be that which one is not." The sentence sounded involved enough to be a word-for-word translation from the Basque. "I think the madman is the brains of the pair."

"But the other does all the talking and carries the powder—"

"Of course," said Pablo. "As I said, they are clever."

I made a great show of waking up half an hour later, yawning, stretching, having a moment's trouble orienting myself, then swinging down from the hay cart and walking alongside the donkey. I wondered how close Vicente had come to drawing a red line on my throat.

"When we cross into Andorra," Pablo said, "you will want us to carry the powder for you."

"Perhaps."

"Ah, it is necessary."

"Perhaps. If we are under the straw, we will be safe, will we not?"

"One would hope so."

"Then why should not the powder be safe with us?"

His explanation was involved and, I think, purposely unconvincing. If we were discovered, he said, he could bribe a guard to overlook the fact. But if the powder were found, there would be trouble, and so it would be better to let him take it. It would, he assured me, be quite safe in his hands.

"Are we close to the border?"

"Very close. An hour, perhaps two."

I went back to the wagon. When we approached the Andorran border, Pablo stopped the cart again and made us burrow ourselves underneath the hay. He asked for the powder.

"If they search you," I said, "and find the powder,

you will be in great difficulty. But if they search us and find it, you can deny that you knew what we carried and thus save yourself from trouble."

He let me outfumble him for the check. He and Vicente piled hay on us, and we lay there under the smelly hay while the wagon started up again. Esteban was still half asleep and very much confused. At first he tried to fight his way free of the hay. I finally managed to calm him down, but he obviously didn't like it.

"I do not trust those men," he said. "Do you?"

"Of course not."

"No? I think they are thieves and entirely ruthless. I think they would kill us without a second thought."

"I agree."

"You do?"

"Vicente was going to kill you while you slept. But Pablo would not let him."

"He was going to kill me?"

"With a knife," I said. "He was going to slit your throat."

"Mother of God—"

"But it's all right now," I assured him.

And it was. The border was easily crossed. Pablo and Vicente evidently did quite a bit of smuggling and were well known at that station. The wagon passed through without incident, continued on through the postage stamp republic of Andorra, and cleared French Customs on the other side. I felt a little sad about this. I was one of the few Americans actually to travel to Andorra and I saw nothing whatsoever of it, spending my entire passage through the country at the bottom of a load of hay. When one could neither see anything nor understand the language, I thought, one might as well have stayed home and watched it all on television.

*   *   *

I was a little worried about ditching Pablo and Vicente, but it turned out that they were more anxious to get away from us than we were to see the last of them. We had a ceremonial drink of wine together, and they went their way, and we went ours, walking north into France. In the first café we came to we ordered breakfast, and I opened the attaché case and drew out the little tin of face powder.

"I do not understand," said Esteban.

"I bought this in Zaragoza," I explained. "I bought a tin of face powder and spilled it out and replaced the powder with confectioner's sugar and crushed aspirin. It was supposed to taste like heroin, and I guess it passed the test. You see, they would hardly have smuggled us across the border out of charity. There had to be profit in it for them, and a tin of heroin would represent a fairly elaborate profit."

He was nodding eagerly.

"Do you remember when Pablo left the hut in Sort to obtain supplies? He ran off to buy a can of face powder. Then while you slept they switched cans with us. So we started with face powder and now we wind up with face powder." I gave the can to Esteban. "For you," I said. "For your salon in Paris."

"Then we never had any heroin?"

"Of course not."

"Oh. And they do not have heroin now, do they?"

"They have a dime's worth of sugar and a nickel's worth of crushed aspirin. That's all."

"Ah."

"If they sniff it," I said, "they're in for a big disappointment."

*C*hapter 11

*I*t was almost impossible to explain to Esteban that we were not going to Paris together. He insisted that brothers such as we could not be separated and he ultimately began to weep and tear at his hair. I did not want to go to Paris. There was a man I had to see in Grenoble, near the Italian border. I tried to put Esteban on a Paris train, but he would have no part of it. I had to come with him, he insisted. Without me he would be lost.

The irritating thing was that I knew he was telling the truth. Without me he definitely would be lost, and I couldn't help feeling an annoying sense of responsibility for him. For a time I toyed with the thought of taking him with me. This, though, was plainly out of the question. He had been enough of a liability in his native land. In Italy, in Yugoslavia, in Turkey, he would be a fatal burden.

When I had recovered the gold, when I had dispatched the mysterious documents to the proper place, when I had somehow cleared myself with the Irish police and the Turkish police and the American authorities and whatever other national bureaus had developed an interest in me, then I could find some way to take care of Esteban. In the meanwhile he would survive. He was too mad to get into serious trouble.

And so we boarded a train to Paris, Esteban and I. We got on the train at Foix, and I got off it at Toulouse and took another train east to Nîmes and a bus northeast to Grenoble. M. Gerard Monet must have already received the cryptic note I'd sent him from Ireland. I went to his home. His wife said that he was at his wine shop—it was not quite noon—and told me how to find him. I walked to the shop and introduced myself as Pierre, who had written from Ireland. He put a finger to his lips, walked past me to the door, closed it, locked and bolted it, drew a window shade, and took me behind the counter.

He was a dusty man in a dusty shop, his hair long and uncombed, his eyes a brilliant blue. "You have come," he said. "Tell me only what I must do. That is all."

"My name is—"

He held up one hand, corded with dark blue veins. "But no, do not tell me. A man can repeat only what he knows, and I wish to know nothing. My father was of the movement. My great-grandfather fell at Waterloo. Did you know that?"

"No."

"For all my life I have been of the movement. I have watched. I have listened. Will anything come of it? In my lifetime? Or ever? I do not know. I will be honest with you, I doubt that anything will come of it. But who is to say? They tell me the days of Empire are over for all time. The glory of France, eh? But I do what there is for me to do. Whatever is requested, Gerard Monet will perform what he is capable of performing. But tell me nothing of yourself or your mission. When I drink, I talk. When I talk, I tell too much. What I do not know I can tell no one, drunk or sober. You understand?"

"Yes."

"What do you require?"

"Entry to Italy."

"You have papers?"

"Perhaps."

"Pardon?"

"I don't know whether or not they're valid. I'd rather slip across the border, if that can be arranged."

"It can. It can, and with ease."

He picked up the telephone, put through a call, talked rapidly in a low voice, then turned to me. "You can leave in an hour?"

"Yes."

"In an hour my nephew will come to drive you to the border. There are places where one may cross. First we shall lunch together."

"You are kind."

"I know how to serve. The Monets have always known how to serve. Do you go to Corsica? No, do not tell me. I have never been to Corsica. Let us have lunch."

We had rolls and cheese and some rather good wine. Afterward Monet poured cognac for each of us. We raised our glasses to toast the eternal memory of Napoleon Bonaparte and pray for a speedy restoration of his line to power in France. I made my brandy last. He had three more before his nephew arrived.

"A grand occupation for such as me," he said, waving a hand to include the shop. "Eh? A wine shop for a drunkard, a dusty shop for a man with impossible dreams. You will not tell them that I drink?"

"No."

"You are a good man. I drink up all the profits. I talk when I drink. Tell me nothing."

"All right."

The nephew was my age, dark, sullen, handsome,

and uncommunicative. He drove a Citroën. The car was silent, the ride soft, the countryside beautiful under a hot sun. The nephew did not ask me who I was or why I wanted to go to Italy. He did not seem to care.

"The old man is crazy," he said once.

I did not answer.

"He thinks he's Napoleon."

"Oh?"

"Crazy," he said. And that was all he said for the rest of the ride. He stopped the car finally at the side of the road—a narrow road winding through hilly country. From here, he said, I would have to walk cross-country. He pointed the way through the fields and asked me if I had something with me to cut the wires. I did not. He grumbled, rummaged through the trunk of the Citroën, and found a pair of wire-cutting pliers.

"I don't suppose you'll be able to return these," he said. "They're not cheap, you know. Every time the old bastard calls me, it costs me money. He must think I'm made of it."

I offered to pay him for the pliers. He said they cost twenty-five francs, a little over five dollars. This was obviously untrue, but I paid the money, and he left without a word.

I walked about a mile through the countryside to the six-foot barbed-wire fence dividing France and Italy. I looked in both directions and saw no sign of life. I cut out a large section of the fence and crawled through. It seemed overly simple. I got to my feet in Italy, flipped the pliers back into France, and looked around vacantly, waiting for whistles to blow or sirens to sound or bullets to whine overhead. Nothing happened. I turned, finally, and walked on into Italy.

*　　*　　*

A farmer in a light pickup truck drove me as far as Torino, where I caught a train to Milan. With Mussolini gone, the Italian trains no longer ran on time. Mine was an hour late leaving Torino and lost another hour on the way to Milan. I left it in Milan and thought about buying a car. I had no contacts in Italy that lay anywhere near my route to Udine near the Yugoslav border. A secondhand Fiat would cut the distance and might be safer. I could drive without stopping and no one would notice my face, as might happen on a train.

But did one need a driver's license to purchase a car? I was not sure. I found a dealer's lot on the northern outskirts of Milan and looked at several cars. The cheapest was 175,000 lire, a little less than three hundred dollars. I could afford to pay for it in Swiss francs. I presented my Swiss passport as identification, and the dealer took it into the shop with him. I patted the little Fiat on the fender. With luck, I thought, the car could be a tremendous asset. I would have the registration and the passport and I might be able to drive it right across the Yugoslav border without any difficulty. That would cut down the risk considerably, leaving me only one tricky border to cross—the one into Turkey. And by that time I would be able to think of something. I was sure of it.

But the dealer seemed to be taking an unduly long time with my passport. I walked over to the office and saw him crouched over his desk, talking on the telephone.

There was something furtive in his manner. I moved closer and caught a few words. "Swiss passport . . . Henri Boehm . . . the one you are looking for, the fugitive—"

I ran like a thief.

*　　*　　*

In downtown Milan I picked up a copy of the Paris edition of the *New York Herald Tribune* and learned what all the fuss was about. The passports were a dead issue, worthless now, a liability. Someone had connected me to the tall man who had been shot down in Dublin. The paper didn't spell it out but explained that the fugitive Evan Michael Tanner had stolen important government documents in Ireland and was thought to be making his escape through continental Europe. They knew I had left Dublin under the false American passport and knew I had changed money under the British one at Madrid.

In an alleyway I destroyed the other two passports. I broke the cases open, tore the printed matter into scraps, and tossed the scraps to the winds. I was about to do the same to the remaining passport, the one for Mustafa Ibn Ali, but it seemed to me that there might be a use for it sometime, perhaps in Yugoslavia. One never knew.

The newspaper article described the black attaché case I was carrying, so I had to rid myself of that, too. I didn't know where to throw it away, so I sold it in a secondhand store for a handful of lire. The money was scarcely enough to matter, but I was getting to the point where money mattered, even small amounts. The damned car dealer still had my Swiss francs, and I was starting to run out of cash.

I buttoned under my shirt the packet of papers I had taken from the attaché case and walked to the railroad station. Would they be watching it? I had no doubt that they would. They had had a call from the car dealer, and I had confirmed his suspicions by bolting like a bat out of hell. I stopped on the way and bought a change of clothes, a hat, heavy shoes. At least I no longer matched the description the dealer would have given them.

I caught a train for Venice without incident. I bought my ticket on the train, locked myself in my compartment and read the rest of the *Herald Tribune.* The sky was dark by the time we reached Venice. I was glad of this. I felt safer in the dark, less conspicuous.

Another bus took me northeast to Udine. I felt as though I had been traveling forever, moving endlessly and to no great purpose. Plane, bus, train, hay wagon, train, bus, car, truck, train, bus—I wondered why I hadn't flown from Dublin to Venice in the first place and cut out all the island-hopping in between. The answer, of course, was that I had wanted to get out of Dublin as quickly as possible. But I seemed to be doing everything wrong. I had put them on my trail all over again by stupidly flashing the Swiss passport in Milan. They probably realized I was on my way to Turkey. If nothing else, they obviously knew I was in Italy and would be able to guess that I was heading east.

And all I could do in the meanwhile was run from burrow to burrow like a frightened rabbit. I had the names of some Croat exiles in Udine, but I couldn't be sure they would help me. And if they did, what then? They could sneak me into Yugoslavia, and I could shuttle around from one band of Balkan conspirators to another. This time, though, I would be doing it all behind the Iron Curtain, where every third conspirator was an agent for the secret police.

Marvelous.

I wished, suddenly, that I could sleep. Just close my eyes and let everything go blank for a while. I had been running too long, I realized. I needed some time to let loose. That was one of the troubles with being able to live without sleep. Because one never got sleepy, one now and then failed to realize that one was tired. I had been going without any real rest since . . . when? Since the few hours of relative rest in the attic hideaway at the Dolans' house in Croom. And how long ago was that?

It was hard to calculate. It seemed as though the whole span of time was only one endless day, but that wasn't right. I'd been at the Dolans' one night, spent the next night skulking around Dublin waiting for the plane, spent the night after that waiting for Vicente to cut my throat in the hay cart, and now it was night again.

No wonder it was beginning to get to me.

Ljudevit Starcevic had a small farm outside of Udine. He grew vegetables, had a small grape arbor, and kept a herd of goats. When an independent Yugoslavia had been carved out of the Austro-Hungarian Empire at the close of the First World War, he had joined Stefan Radic's Croat Peasant Party. In 1925 Radic abandoned separatism and joined the central government. Starcevic did not. He and other Croatian extremists fought the central regime. Some were killed. Starcevic, who was very young at the time, was imprisoned, escaped, and eventually wound up in Italy.

He was astonished when I spoke to him in Croat.

He lived alone, he told me. His wife was dead, his children had married Italians and moved away. He lived with his goats and saw hardly anyone. And he wanted—desperately—to talk.

He fed me a dish of meat and rice. We sat together and drank plum brandy and talked of the future of Croatia.

"You have come from our homeland?"

"No," I said.

"You go there?"

"Yes."

"You must watch out for the Serbs. They are treacherous."

"I understand."

"How will you go?"

I explained that I had to cross the border. He wanted to know if I planned to start a revolution. It was difficult to keep from laughing aloud. There would never be a revolution, I was tempted to tell him. The little splinters of Balkan nationalism were almost entirely in exile, and the few who remained to plot and scheme against their governments were bent old men like Ljudevit Starcevic, himself.

But of course I did not say this. His was a noble madness and a special form of lunacy that I was happy to share with him. One may, in this happy world, believe what one wishes to believe. And it pleased me to believe that one day Croatia would throw off the yoke of the Belgrade Government and take her rightful place among the nations, just as it pleased me to believe that Prince Rupert would one day dispossess Betty Saxe-Coburg from Buckingham Palace, that the Irish Republican Army would liberate the Six Counties, that Cilician Armenia would be again reborn and, for that matter, that the earth was flat.

"I will not start a revolution," I said.

"Ah." His eyes were downcast.

"Not this time."

"But soon?"

"Perhaps."

His leathery face creased in a smile. "And now? What do you plan this trip, Vanec?"

"There are men I must see. Plans to be made."

"Ah."

"But first I must cross the border."

He thought this over for some time. "It is possible," he admitted. "I have been back myself. Not many times, you understand, because it is, of course, very dangerous for me. I am a hunted man in my native land. The police are constantly on the lookout for me. They know that I am dangerous. It would be death for me to be caught there."

It was entirely possible, I thought, that no one in the Yugoslav Government so much as knew his name.

"But I have been back. I go once in a very great while to see my people. It is a land of great beauty, my Croatia. But you know this, of course."

"Of course."

"But the border," he said, and put his face in his hands and closed his eyes in thought. "It is possible. I can take you myself. I am old, I move more slowly than I did in my youth, but it is no matter. I must take you, do you understand? Because there is no one else I could trust with the task!"

He stuffed tobacco into the bowl of a pipe and lit it with a wooden match. He puffed solemnly on the pipe, then set it down on the scarred wooden top of the table.

"I can take you," he said.

"Good."

"But not tonight. Not for several days. This is— what? Saturday night, yes?"

"Yes."

"Tomorrow is Sunday. That is no good. Then Monday, then Tuesday. Tuesday night will be good."

"It will?"

"Yes. Tuesday is the best night to cross the border. There is a stretch of the border just a few kilometers from here where there are three guards. Always three guards, walking back and forth. It is allowed to cross only at the Customs stations, you see. And at the rest of the border where one is not allowed to cross there are always guards, and here there are three guards."

He relit the pipe. "But on Tuesday," he said triumphantly, "there will be only two guards!"

"Why is that so?"

"It is always so. Who knows why? Whenever I cross the border, I do so on Tuesday, Vanec."

"And on Tuesday—"

"On Tuesday two men must do the work of three. They cannot cover the space. Believe me, I know how to get you to Croatia. My only worry is your fate when you arrive. Never trust the Serbs. Trust a snake before a Serb, do you follow me?"

I didn't entirely, but I said I did.

"But tonight is Saturday," said Ljudevit Starcevic. "Saturday, Sunday, Monday, Tuesday. You must stay here until then. It will be easy for you. It will be safe here. Who would look for you here? No one. You will eat, you will sleep, you will walk in the fields with the goats and sit with me by the fire. Do you play dominoes?"

"Yes."

"Then we will play dominoes. And you will get as much rest as possible so that you will be fresh and at ease when it is time for you to return to our homeland."

Saturday, Sunday, Monday, Tuesday, I would have to stay in one place all that time, marking time when I might otherwise be working my way inch by inch through Yugoslavia and into Turkey. For all those vital days I would be stuck on a farm in the northeast corner of Italy with nothing to do but eat and drink and rest and read and play dominoes.

It sounded wonderful.

Chapter 12

Clouds filled the sky all Tuesday afternoon. The night was black as a coal mine, moonless and starless. Around eight o'clock old Starcevic and I set out for the border. I carried a leather satchel he had given me. In it was a loaf of bread, several wedges of ripe cheese, a flask of plum brandy, and the inevitable mysterious documents that were my last souvenir of Ireland. We walked along narrow mountain paths. There was lightning and thunder in the west, but the storm was a long way off, and it was not raining where we were.

When we approached the border, Starcevic drew me down in a clump of shrubbery. "Now we must be very quiet," he whispered. "In a few moments the border guard will pass us. You see that tree? If you climb it, you can get over the fence. I have climbed it and I am an old man, so you will be over it with no difficulty. We will wait until the guard passes and then we will wait five minutes, no longer, and then you will climb the tree and jump over the fence. It is not Croatia on the other side, you know. It is Slovenia."

"I know."

"Trust a snake before a Slovene. Tell them nothing. But in Croatia you will meet your friends."

"Of course."

"But why do I tell you these things?" He laughed

softly. "You could tell me more than I could tell you, for it is you who will start the revolution."

"I—"

"Oh, I know, I know. You must not say as much, not even to me. But I know, Vanec. I know."

He fell silent. I waited, my eyes on the tree and the fence beyond it. The tree did not look all that easy to climb. There was a branch that extended over the fence, and I saw that it would be possible to move along the branch and jump clear of the fence. It would also be possible to make a very attractive target on the branch, outlined against the sky. At least the sky was dark and, according to Starcevic, there would be worlds of time once the sentry had passed.

After a few moments we saw the sentry pass. He was tall enough to play professional basketball. He wore high laced boots and a severely tailored uniform and carried a rifle. In my mind I saw him swing the rifle surely and easily, like a gunner in a movie short on skeet-shooting, zeroing in on a man poised on the branch of a tree, squeezing off an easy shot and dropping his prey.

We waited five long minutes. Then Starcevic touched my shoulder and pointed at the tree. I ran to it, tossed my leather satchel high over the fence, and shinnied up the tree. I climbed out onto the proper branch and felt it bend under my weight, but it held me, and I moved out until I was clear of the boundary fence. I had the horrible feeling that a gun barrel was trained on me and I waited for a shot to pierce the night. No shot came. I caught hold of the branch with my hands, let my feet swing down, then let go and dropped a few yards to the ground. I found the satchel, snatched it up, and started walking.

So that was the Iron Curtain, I thought. A stretch of barbed wire one could pass over simply by shinnying up a tree. A hazardous obstacle for James Bond and his cohorts but child's play for that great Croatian revolutionary, Evan Tanner.

I felt wonderful. The days and nights at Starcevic's farm had done me worlds of good. Merely staying in one place for a few days rested me, and the security of knowing that I was safe, that I could eat and drink and lie down without constantly looking over my shoulder for police in one shape or another was a luxury to which I had recently become unaccustomed. Starcevic himself was a decent enough companion, pleasant enough to talk with and agreeably silent when I did not feel like talking. He worried that I was not getting enough sleep, as I always stayed up after he went to bed and managed to be awake before he rose in the morning. But he was so happy to have someone around to speak Croat to him and play dominoes with him that he was careful not to press or pry.

Now, rested and recovered, I felt equal to the challenge of Yugoslavia. It could be both easy and hard at once; it was a police state, on the one hand, and it was at the same time an utter gold mine of political extremists. The national groups that made up Yugoslavia were by no means a homogenized blend. Each province had dreams of independence, and in each province there were men whom I knew, men to whom I had written those cryptic notes. It was easy to construct a route that would lead safely and surely down into Bulgaria and from there to Turkey. I had entered Slovenia. I would move south and east through Croatia and Slavonia to Vukovar on the Danube—where I was awaited—then south through Serbia, stopping in Kragujevac, and on to Djakovica in Kosovo-Metohija, and stopping finally in any of several towns in Macedonia before turning east for the Bulgarian border. The whole trip would run around five hundred miles, and I might have to take my time, but I could expect to be sheltered every step of the way.

And there would be no Estebans in Yugoslavia, no inept conspirators. An inept conspirator in Yugoslavia very speedily found his way into prison. These men of mine might lead equally futile lives, but they would be professionals in their futility. I could count on them.

By dawn Wednesday I had reached the Slovenian city of Ljubljana. There a displaced Serbian teacher took me into his house, fed me breakfast, and took me to a friend who let me ride to Zagreb in the back of his truck. The ride was bumpy but quick. In Zagreb, Sandor Kofalic fed me roasted lamb and locked me in his cellar with a bottle of sweet wine while he rounded up a Croat separatist who had landed a berth as a minor functionary in the local Communist Party. I never learned the man's name; he didn't mention it, and I had the sense not to ask it. He provided me with a travel pass that would let me ride the trains as far as Belgrade (bypassing Vukovar). I would have to be careful in Belgrade, he counseled me, and I should not attempt to take the trains any further south, but, if I had friends, I would find my way readily enough.

In Belgrade I had dinner with Janos Papilov. He did not have a car, he told me, but a friend of his did, and perhaps he could borrow it. I waited at his house and played cards with his wife and father-in-law while he went to hunt up transportation. He came back with a car, and late at night we set out. He drove me sixty miles to Kragujevac and apologized that he could go no farther. Like the others I had met, he did not ask where I was going or why I was going there. He knew only that I was a comrade and in trouble and assumed that I was going someplace important and had something important to do there. That was enough to satisfy him.

I stayed the night in Kragujevac with an old widow who had a son in America. She told me that much and nothing more, asked no questions, and told me to keep away from the windows. I did this. In the morning, before the sky was light, I left her house and walked south on a road out of town. The woman had no transportation available and was unable to arrange any for me, so I took the road south, picked up a ride with a farmer as far as the little town of Kraljevo, and there caught up with a neat relay network that took me step-by-step down to Djakovica. Nine men combined to carry me a little over a hundred miles. Each took me ten or twelve or fifteen miles on horseback, turned me over to yet another man, and returned home.

By nightfall I was in Tetovo in Macedonia. And there I felt safer than ever. The whole province of Macedonia is peppered with revolutionaries and conspirators. The ghost of the IMRO, the Internal Macedonian Revolutionary Organization, had never been entirely laid. In the years before the First World War the IMRO had its own underground government in the Macedonian hills, ran its own law courts, and dispensed its own revolutionary justice. Its spies and agents ran amok throughout the Balkans. And, though generations have passed since the cry of "Macedonia for the Macedonians" first echoed through that rocky would-be nation, the IMRO lives on. It may be found in every hamlet of Macedonia. It is listed even now on the U.S. attorney general's list of subversive organizations.

Of course I am a member.

In Tetovo I stopped at a café for a glass of resinous wine. I had gradually changed my clothing in the course of my pilgrimage through Yugoslavia, and I was now wearing the same sort of garb as most of the men in the café. I received a few glances, perhaps because I was a stranger, but no one paid much attention to me. I drank the wine, asked directions to the address I had, and headed for Todor Prolov's house.

It was a smallish hut at the end of a drab and narrow street off the main thoroughfare, on the southeast edge of downtown Tetovo. Broken panes of glass in the casement windows had been patched with newspaper. Two dogs, thin and yellow-eyed, slept in the doorway and ignored me.

I knocked at the door.

The girl who opened the door had an opulent body and blonde hair like spun silk. She held a chicken bone in one hand.

"Does Todor Prolov live here?"

She nodded.

"I wrote him a letter," I said. "My name is Ferenc."

Her eyes, large and round to begin with, now turned to saucers. She grabbed my arm, pulled me inside. "Todor," she shouted, "he is here! The one who wrote you! Ferenc! The American!"

A horde of people clustered around me. From the center of the mob, Todor Prolov pushed forward to face me. He was a short man with a twisted face and unruly brown hair and a pair of shoulders like the entire defensive line of the Green Bay Packers. He reached out both hands and gripped my upper arms. When he spoke, he shouted.

"You wrote me a letter?" he bellowed.

"Yes."

"Signed Ferenc?"

"Yes."

"But you are Tanner! Evan Tanner!"

"Yes."

"From America?"

"Yes."

A murmur of excitement ran through the group around us. Todor released my arms, stepped back, studied me, then moved closer again.

"We have been waiting for you," he said. "Ever since your letter arrived, all of Tetovo has been in a state of excitement. Excitement!"

Again his hands fastened on my biceps. "And now the big question," he roared. "Are you with us?"

"Of course," I said, puzzled.

"With IMRO?"

"Of course."

He stepped forward and caught me in a bear hug, lifting me up off my feet and leaving me quite breathless. He set me down, spun around, and shouted at the crowd.

"America is with us!" he roared. "You have heard him speak, have you not? America will aid us! America supports Macedonia for the Macedonians! America will help us crush the tyranny of the Belgrade dictatorship! America backs our cause! America knows our history of resistance to oppression! America is with us!"

Behind me the streets had suddenly filled up with Macedonians. I saw men holding guns and women with bricks and pitchforks. Everyone was shouting.

"The time has come!" Todor shrieked. "Raise the barricades! March on the homes of the tyrants! Root out and destroy the oppressors! Give no quarter! Rise and die for Macedonia!"

A child rushed by me holding a bottle in his hand. There was a rag stuffed into the neck of it. The rag smelled of gasoline.

I turned to the girl who had opened the door for me. "What's happening? What's going on?"

"But of course you know. You are a part of it."

"A part of what?"

She hugged me with joy. "A part of our triumph," she said. "A part of our finest hour. A part of—"

"What?"

"Our revolution," she said.

Chapter 13

*T*he street had gone mad. There were so many guns going off that they no longer sounded like gunfire. It was too much to be real, more like a fireworks display on the Fourth of July. To the north a row of houses was already in flames. A police car roared past us, and men dropped to their knees to fire at it. One shot burst a tire. The car swung out of control, plowed off the street into a shop front. The police jumped out, guns ready, and the men in the street shot them down.

The girl was at my side. "They're crazy," I said. "They'll all be killed."

"Those who die will die in glory."

"They can't stand off an army—"

"But America will help us."

I stared at her.

"You said America would help. You told Todor—"

"I told him I was behind his cause. That is all."

"But you are with the CIA, are you not?"

"I'm *running from* the CIA."

"Then, who will help my people?"

"I don't know."

Two blocks down the street a canvas-topped truck careened around the corner and pulled to a stop. Uniformed troops spilled from it. Some of them had machine guns. They crouched at the side of the truck and began firing into the crowd of Macedonians. I saw a woman cut in two by machine-gun fire. She fell, and a baby tumbled from her arms, and another blast of gunfire tore the child's head off.

Shrieking, a young girl heaved a homemade cannister bomb into the nest of soldiers. The gunfire ceased. Two of the soldiers staggered free of the truck, clutching at their wounds, and a ragged volley of shots from the rooftops cut them down.

Sirens blared to the north. The whole town was alive with the fury of the uprising. The girl was still at my side, but I wasn't paying attention to the words she said.

Revolution—

I had told Starcevic there would be no revolution. Not in his beloved Croatia, not anywhere. I was, after all, no revolutionary, no *agent provocateur*. I was simply a treasure hunter headed for a cache of gold. But it was I who had sparked this, and it was, after all, a revolution. Mills bombs, Molotov cocktails, barricades thrown up in the streets, bursts of gunfire, the screams of the wounded—these were not sound effects, not bits of the backdrop of a movie, but the sounds of a popular rising, a revolution.

When one has long been conditioned to respond in a certain fashion to a certain set of stimuli, one does not think things out. One reacts and glories in it.

I reacted.

A police van had piled up at the barricade closing the south end of the block. A trio of uniformed troopers had taken up positions behind the barricade and were firing at us. Two had rifles, one a Sten gun. I grabbed up a brick from the ground and heaved it at them. It fell far short.

Their fire came our way. I ran forward, toward the

source of the firing. A youth ran beside me, pistol in hand. More shots rang out. The youth dropped, moaning, wounded in the thigh.

I grabbed up his pistol.

I kept running. The Sten gun swung around and pointed at me. I fired without aiming and was astonished to see the policeman spill forward, a massive hole in his throat. His blood washed out of him and coated the piled-up bedsteads and furniture of the improvised barricade. One of the other police fired at me. The bullet brushed my jacket. I ran toward him and shot him in the chest. The third one shoved a rifle in my face and pulled the trigger. The gun jammed. I clubbed him aside and kicked him in the face. He was reaching for another gun when I lowered the pistol and blew off the back of his head.

A cheer went up behind me. The rebels had fired a public building in the center of town. I grabbed up the Sten gun of the first cop I had killed and pushed forward with the crowd. For four blocks almost every house we passed was in flames. In the middle of the city, we pressed in around the police station. A small force of police and soldiers had barricaded themselves inside the stationhouse. They were firing into the crowd from the windows and lobbing grenades down amongst us. I saw the girl who had been at Todor's house putting a torch to the front door. The flames leaped. A band of men were heaving Molotov cocktails into a second-story window. The blaze spread in several places, and the crowd dropped back out of range to let the fire have its head.

We shot them down as they came out. There must have been two dozen of them, not counting the ones who never got out the door.

In the public square, Todor proclaimed the Independent and Sovereign Republic of Macedonia. "Historic birthright" and "sever the shackles of Serbian oppression" were phrases that kept recurring. It was, all in all, a good proclamation. He paused once, and part of the crowd, thinking he had finished, began to cheer, but he picked up again, and the cheering died down. Then he did finish the speech, and a ground swell of exhilarated applause burst from the mass of people, and for a thin fraction of a moment I actually thought the revolution would succeed.

The Independent and Sovereign Republic of Macedonia, while unrecognized by the other independent and sovereign nations of the earth, did endure in fact for four hours, twenty-three minutes, and an indeterminate number of seconds. Thinking back, I cannot help viewing this lifespan as an enormous moral victory. It was at least five times the duration I would have predicted for the Republic, although it fell far short of Todor's expectations—he had announced at one point that Free Macedonia would endure, as was claimed for the Third Reich, for a minimum of a thousand years.

Those four hours were as active as any I had ever spent. After the police station fell to us, we still had to conduct mop-up operations throughout the town. It was necessary, for example, to dispatch a delegation to rouse the mayor from his bed, take him out of his house, and hang him from the tree in front of his front porch. It was also necessary to rush the town's small Serbian quarter and massacre the inhabitants thereof. I was fortunate enough to miss out on both the hanging and the pogrom, however. During this stage of the revolution I was cloistered with Todor and Annalya.

Annalya was his sister, with blonde hair and huge eyes and hour-glass body. The three of us—a troika? a triumvirate? a junta? no matter—were to plan the course of the revolution.

"You shall not return to America," Todor insisted. "You shall stay here forever in Macedonia. I will make you my prime minister."

"Todor—"

"I will also make you my brother-in-law. You will marry Annalya. You like her?"

"Todor, what do we do when they send in the tanks?"

"What tanks?"

"They used tanks in Budapest in fifty-six. What can your people do against tanks?"

He thought this over. "What did they do in Budapest?"

"They used Molotov cocktails on them."

He brightened. "Then we will do the same!"

"It didn't work in Budapest. The revolt was crushed."

"Oh."

"The rebels were shot down by the hundreds. The leaders were executed."

While he tried to think of a reply to this dismal bit of news a man burst in with some information that took the edge off what I had said. Reports were coming in of sympathetic risings throughout Macedonia. Skopje, the provincial capital, was in flames. Kumanovo had gone to the rebels almost without a shot. There were rumors of rebellion in Britolj and Prilep in the south.

Todor rocked me with another bear hug. "You see? It is not one city in arms, like your Budapest. It is a nation taking its place among nations. It is an entire people rising as one man to throw off their chains and capture their freedom. And we shall triumph!"

Annalya and I left him. We ran around town, planning the defense of Tetovo. If it were true that other cities were in arms, we might have a little more time to prepare for the assault from Belgrade. We ranged barricades around the entire town, blocking off every road in and out of it and concentrating the bulk of our defenses across the main road in the north and the smaller roads immediately to either side of it. I was fairly certain the initial assault would come from that direction. If we were properly prepared, we might be able to break even in the first attack.

After that, when the tanks came down and the fighter planes dived overhead, was something I did not want to think about.

"Ferenc?"

"What?"

"Do we have any chance?"

I looked at her. I decided that she wanted me to lie to her, so I told her that there was a good chance we could win if every man fought as hard as he could.

"Ferenc?"

"What?"

"Tell me the truth."

"There is no chance, Annalya."

"I thought not. We will all be killed?"

"Perhaps. They may not want a massacre. The Russians got a fairly bad press after Hungary. They may just kill the leaders."

"Like Todor?"

I didn't answer her.

"It would be horrid if we lost and they spared him."

"I do not understand."

She smiled. "My brother wishes to be a hero. He is a hero already. He has fought like a hero and he will fight like a hero again when the troops arrive. It is only fitting that he die like a hero. Do you understand?"

"Yes."

"Where will the worst of the fighting be?"

"In the center."

"You are certain?"

I nodded. "The other streets are too narrow for heavy traffic. Even if they want to spread out for strategic reasons, the heavy weapons and the mass of men will come right down the center."

"Then I must be certain that Todor is here," she said. "In the center. May it please God that he dies before he learns that we are to be defeated."

I had spotters stationed a mile out on the main road to the north. When the revolution was just a hair under two hours old, they rode back full speed to announce that the troops were on their way. I asked what sort of vehicles were coming, but they had not noticed. In their eagerness to bring the news to us as fast as possible, they had neglected to determine just what sort of troops were headed our way or how many of them we could expect.

The first wave, as it turned out, was an afterthought. Evidently a mass of troops had been dispatched to the capital, and some major had decided it might be a good idea to find out what was happening in Tetovo. They sent four truckloads of infantry and two units of mobile artillery at us, and that wasn't enough to storm the city. We were properly deployed behind our barricades, we were fairly well armed, and we fought like cornered rats. The government troops threw everything they had at our center, and I told our men on the east and west to move in and engulf them.

We brought it off. The two small cannons never got to do us much damage. A batch of our sharpshooters knocked off the two gun crews before more than four or five rounds had been fired, and the few shells that looped over the barricades at us had little effect. Bottles of flaming gas had the trucks in flames before the men had finished pouring out of them. We suffered casualties—over a dozen dead, almost as many wounded. But we completely destroyed the government forces.

Half an hour later they brought in an attacking force five times the strength of the first, and they rolled right over us.

"The same thing you do. House-sitting."

"*You're* the house-sitter? Agency didn't say you were coming."

"Agency didn't send me. I'm in business for myself."

Gaylord looked Serge over. "I'll need references."

"References? Sure." Serge pointed up the street. "Jim."

"Jim?"

"Your new neighbor. Three houses up."

"Oh, the Davenports." He nodded. "Nice people. Only talked a couple times. Jim's a little on the quiet side, but Martha seems like a wonderful woman."

"She is."

"Where do you know Jim from?"

"Uh . . . we meet each week. We're in the same *club*."

"You and Jim belong to the club?" said Wainscotting. "*I* belong to the club. Living on this side of the island, I should have known Jim was a member. Wonder why he didn't tell me?"

"Are you serious?" said Serge. "It's not exactly the kind of thing you talk about."

"Couldn't agree more," said Wainscotting. "Can't stand this new wealth that puts on the dog."

"Those fuckers!"

Gaylord laughed. "No shit . . . Say, I like you. If they accepted you in the club, no need for any background checks. Their membership committee's worse than the FBI." He finished his plantation drink and smacked Serge on the shoulder. "Let's go inside."

They entered through a front door with a giant heron etched into the glass. "What are you drinking?"

"White grapefruit," said Serge. "Chilled, not iced."

"Loosen up. I got Chivas, Stoli, Johnny Walker Blue."

"I drink *after* business."

"Good for you. Luckily I'm finished with business for life." Gaylord poured himself a generous Belvedere vodka martini. "Made most of mine in the stock market. Good broker, if you know what I mean."

"A little Martha Stewart birdie in your ear?"

Gaylord winked. "How'd you make yours?"

"Currency conversion."

"Now you *really* got my respect. I don't have the stones for that kind of action. The least little fluctuation in the dollar and you're ruined."

"That's why I only work with great big fluctuations."

"Bet you made a lot of money."

"Literally."

Gaylord finished his first martini and began fixing another. "We're a lot alike—have to do the club together sometime."

"Just say the word."

Gaylord dumped ice in a sterling cylinder, capped it and began shaking. "I *love* the club. Why haven't I seen you there? Or Jim?"

"We go Tuesdays."

"You should try Wednesdays. The most tender prime rib in town."

"We just get stale coffee and doughnuts."

"But they're supposed to have stone crab on Tuesday."

"You sure we're talking about the same club?"

"I know, I know. But last year was an exception." Gaylord uncapped the shaker. "With all the staff turnover, you never knew which club you were going to get. Guess they still have some kinks to iron out. I'll talk to Remington. Meantime, switch to Wednesdays. Nothing like a big steak after a round of golf."

"Golf?" said Serge. "I hate the fucking game!"

"What?"

"You'd have to be a complete idiot to play that stupid shit."

"Tell me about it," said Gaylord. "I could murder the guy

who invented the elevated green. But it's an addiction worse than any drug. What are you going to do?"

"Feed the monkey."

Gaylord speared an olive. "Why'd *you* join the club?"

"Deal with aggression."

"Feels like I'm talking to a mirror." Gaylord refilled his martini glass to the brim. "That's why I joined. It's like therapy."

"What do you mean *like*? It *is* therapy."

"No shit. Eighteen holes and I'm a new man." He took a large sip. "Just one question. If you belong to the club and all, why do you need to house-sit?"

"Sold my place on Bayshore a few days ago. Broke my heart, but local prices were beginning to bubble. Rule number one . . ."

". . . Never get emotionally attached to an asset."

"Now I just have the Hamptons spread."

"Cape Cod here."

"But I couldn't give up the club," said Serge. "Figured I'd house-sit until my Realtor finds something else."

Gaylord raised his glass. "To the club."

"The club."

A horn honked.

They looked through the glass front door. Another honk. A rust-eaten Comet at the curb. Rachael behind the wheel. Then she really laid into it for one of those ten-second blasts that got every dog barking for five blocks. Serge slapped himself on the forehead. Gaylord pointed with his cocktail. "Who the hell are those jackasses?"

TWENTY-SEVEN

848 LOBSTER LANE

*D*ing-dong!

Two men stood on a welcome mat.

Jim looked up in awe at the building. "I can't believe this is his *second* home."

Vinny pressed the bell again. "You should see the Pennsylvania compound."

The door opened. Jim's mouth fell. A steamy blonde with black roots in a thong.

"Vinny!"

"Mandy!"

Big hug.

Vinny turned. "I'd like you to meet my friend, Jim. He's faithful, so don't blow him."

Mandy smiled and shook his hand. "Pay no attention to Vin. He's always joking. Nice to meet you."

Jim opened his mouth, but nothing came out.

She looked at Vinny. "Cat got his tongue?"

"The strong silent type." Vinny stepped through the door without invitation. "Is——here?"

"Game room. You know the way."

Jim followed Vinny through the living room, another hot

babe on the couch. She looked up from a mirror and offered Jim a straw. "Booger sugar?"

"What?"

They turned the corner. A long, dark-paneled hallway led to the inner sanctum. Jim checked out the rows of framed *Sports Illustrated* covers that seemed to go on forever. Finally they were standing right in front of it. The Door.

"Here we are," said Vinny. "Holy of Holies."

"——is on the other side?" said Jim.

Vinny knocked hard.

Through the wood: "Shit, who the hell is it?"

"Me, Vinny."

The still-closed door: "Jesus, you scared the hell out of me! Anyone with you?"

"My friend, Jim."

"Who the fuck's Jim?"

"My friend," Vinny whispered sideways: "Don't make any sudden moves until he gets used to you. I think he's been basing."

"What?"

Vinny pounded the door again. "Open up. I'm getting old out here."

The door: "Vinny? . . ."

"What?"

"Is that you?"

"Open the fuckin' door!"

Jim heard fumbling with a variety of locks, bolts and chains. The door opened a slit. A single eyeball scanned back and forth. "You sure it's cool?"

"Let us in, you cocksucker!"

The door opened the rest of the way.

"Vinny!"

"——!"

Hugging time again.

"Got the stuff?"

Vinny reached in the hip pocket of his warm-up suit and tossed a Baggie of light-blue tablets. "Those should bring you down."

The player tossed back a handful of pills and headed for the liquor cabinet.

Vinny gave Jim the all-clear wink. Jim was only two steps inside when his legs stopped working, the same reaction for every first-time visitor to Guy Heaven. The game room was bigger than most banquet halls. Pool table, card table, slot machine in one corner, pinball in another. Full-service bar. Refrigerator with keg tap through the door. Overpadded black leather sofas and La-Z-Boys aimed variously at nine TVs, including the centerpiece eighty-four-inch high-def, currently showing a replay of the '79 Super Bowl, Pittsburgh driving in the red zone. The eighteen speaker surround-sound with subwoofer and ceiling flush-mounts made Jim feel like he was in the middle of the tackle. The smaller televisions featured pornography and live satellite feeds from Vegas sports books.

Then Jim saw it. Vinny could tell his new pal was stricken. "Go ahead and look. Just don't break anything."

Jim walked across an Astroturf putting green until he was standing in front of the trophy wall: built-in shelves and soft recessed spotlights, one for each of the hundred-odd gold statues and plaques and old footballs on tees, dated with stats. Jim could recall every game represented by each of the balls, and even the games represented by little brass plates where football tees were curiously empty. He reached the next wall, the one with sliding glass doors overlooking the football-shaped pool. Thick vertical blinds were drawn tight, keeping the room grotto dark.

Jim peeked outside. His eyes went first to the exquisite sight of Mandy sunning herself next to the diving board. Then he noticed more people. They were on the other side of the seawall, down in the bay, dozens of 'em: canoes and kayaks and rafts and some just treading water in life vests, all quietly staring at the house. They seemed to be waiting for something to happen. Jim slowly pulled a cord for a better look. . . .

"Close those fucking blinds!"

Jim jumped. Vinny rushed over and made the room dark again. "Sudden light overstimulates him."

Serge gritted his teeth and glared out the glass front door at Coleman and Rachael. "Those are my . . . business associates."

Gaylord stared dubiously at the beaten-up vehicle and, for the first time, gave Serge a disappointed look.

"I'm into vintage cars," said Serge. "Haven't had a chance to restore that one yet."

"Ohhh," said Gaylord. "Read an article. Lot of money in that. Why don't you invite your associates in?"

"We're on a tight schedule."

"I insist." He went to the front door and made a big inviting wave. "Don't be strangers."

Two minutes later, Coleman was lining up shot glasses, and Gaylord couldn't pull his eyes off the chick.

"Take a picture," said Rachael. "It'll last longer."

Coleman snapped his fingers. "Over here, moneybags. We're on the clock. Those eight shots are yours; these are mine. One every sixty seconds or until we lose somebody. Go!"

Serge covered his face. "This can't be happening."

Two empty shot glasses slammed on the wet bar. "So, Coleman, what do you do?"

"What do you mean, 'What do I do?'" He grabbed Gaylord's wrist, monitoring the Rolex's second hand. "I hang with Serge."

"Business loyalty. I respect that."

"Now!" said Coleman. Shots went back. Gaylord turned to Rachael. "And what do you do?"

She looked at Serge. "What's with this fuckin' guy? What do I *do*?"

"Gaylord," said Serge. "She runs a profitable website."

"Really? I'd like to see it. We can pull it up in my study."

Serge's arms flew out in alarm. "No! You can't! It's down for repairs!"

"Fuck you!" Rachael shoved Serge in the chest. "Don't ever interfere with my business. . . . Come on, Gayboy."

"Gaylord."

"Whatever." She led him around the corner.

"Hey!" Coleman yelled after him. "You'll lose the game. I'll get your shots."

A door closed.

Coleman grabbed a glass for each hand. "Serge, what a sweet deal! I checked when he wasn't looking. There's all kinds of bottles back here."

Serge pounded a fist on the bar. "Don't you dare screw this up on me!"

"Relax," said Coleman. "The dude parties! Plus he digs Rachael. He may be rich, but he still likes to get his freak on."

A half hour later, shot glasses lay scattered everywhere. Coleman was passed out in the middle of the floor, limbs bent unnaturally like he'd fallen from a balcony. Serge sat on the edge of the sofa, rocking nervously. Rachael came back into the living room, thumbing a thick wad of currency.

Serge stood quickly. "You killed him?"

"Hell no," said Rachael. "He paid me in cash. Didn't want a credit card trail."

Gaylord emerged. "Have to be somewhere. Why don't you familiarize yourself with the place?" He jingled something. "Here are the keys. We leave next Monday."

Before Serge could respond, Gaylord stepped over Coleman and was out the door. A Jag sped off.

The ex-Steelers player was on the main couch, working with a glass bulb. He finished his business and slid the paraphernalia tray under the sofa. "Vinny, let's throw it around."

"You got it, big guy."

The player went to The Wall and grabbed a game ball off a tee.

Jim raced over to Vinny. "Oh my God! We're actually going to play catch?"

"Don't cream your pants."

They exited the sliding doors and walked past the diving board. Vinny nudged Jim. "Mandy's a dish, eh?"

"Who is she?"

"His girlfriend."

"Thought he was married."

"Divorced."

Jim looked back at the house. "Who was that other woman with the cocaine?"

"There's always a million chicks hanging around. But Mandy's his girl."

"Vinny!" yelled the player, smacking the football in his throwing hand. "Go long!"

Vinny began trotting around the far side of the pool. Not a pretty sight. Then he turned and ran backward, waving an arm. "I'm open! I'm open!"

The ball sailed through the air . . . and over the seawall. Pandemonium in the water. Someone floating on a swim noodle raised his prize. "I got it!" The others grumbled, paddling canoes and kayaks back into position.

The player jogged toward the sliding glass door. "I'll get another."

He came back out with a ball from an overtime divisional playoff.

Then Jim couldn't believe his eyes. The player patted the ball and pointed at *him*. "Post route!"

Jim ran along the near side of the pool and watched the ball take flight. It was a timing pattern. Jim kept his eyes skyward as he curled around the shallow end. It seemed to hang forever. Perfect spiral, laces, Wilson. Jim heard heavenly music. Then he saw the ball land in his hands. Unbelievable. He'd just caught a pass from——! He could now die in peace.

But other business first. Jim found himself teetering on the edge of the seawall, twirling his free arm for balance, hopeful eyes below in the water. Then he found equilibrium. The canoe people sagged. Jim strolled back and casually tossed the ball to his hero like he did this every day.

"Nice catch, sport."

Jim fought the urge to weep: *He called me "sport"*!

Vinny's turn again. He ran like a sack of tomatoes. Another ball splashed into the bay, another trip back inside to the trophy shelf.

Jim's turn. Buttonhook pattern, another circus catch. Growing discontent in the water. "Who *is* that guy?"

On it went. For five minutes. Vinny and the player got bored and wanted to call their bookies. They headed toward the house.

For the last hour, Jim had been rehearsing how he would, with the utmost dignity, broach the topic of his interest in the player's career. Not like all the other idiots who claimed to be his number one fan. Jim dashed up to the player. "I'm your number one fan! . . ." He became verbally incontinent, babbling statistics and big games.

Vinny grabbed his shoulder. "Down, puppy."

"No, it's okay." The player's ego inflated. "What's your name, sport?"

He called me "sport" again! "Uh . . ."

The player smiled at Vinny. "He forget his own name?"

"It's Jim," said Vinny. "Hey, Jim. Go get your camera, and I'll take a picture of you two."

"I'll be right back! Don't go anywhere!"

Jim returned with his Pentax and handed it to Vinny. Click, click, click.

Mandy rose from the lounger. "Why don't I get a shot of the three of you?"

Click, click, click. The whole time, Jim: ". . . Remember the Cowboys blizzard game at Three Rivers, when you played the second half with two broken ribs? . . . Or the famous 'drive' against the Dolphins? Ninety-six yards from scrimmage with two to go? . . ."

The player beamed. "Ninety-seven."

". . . The next year you led the league in all-purpose yards. . . ."

"Jim," said Vinny. "Settle down."

"He's fine," said the player, postponing that call to his bookie and grabbing a patio lounger. He slapped the one next to him. "Jim, have a seat. . . . Mandy, baby, can you get some drinks out here?"

It was the beginning of a beautiful friendship: Jim, intricately reciting an entire career and taking more photos; the player, staring up from behind Bulgari sunglasses, envisioning Jim's play-by-plays in the sky and knocking back cocktails strong enough to strip furniture.

". . . You practically invented the press conference no-show! . . ."

The player was in excellent spirits. "Let's barbecue!"

Vinny took over the grill and flipped rib eyes. He insisted on wearing the chef's hat. Jim's inner child grew younger. He followed the player around like a pet, taking copious photos of his every mundane action.

They ended up back on the porch.

Jim advanced his film. "Let me get a picture of you and Mandy."

"Sure."

They posed together. Click. Then the player suddenly threw her over his shoulder. She giggled and kicked her feet. He spanked her bikini bottom. Then he went to set her down on the poolside lounger, but it was more of a fall as they collapsed together and nuzzled. Click, click, click.

Jim went over to the smoking grill.

"Jimbo!" said Vinny, brushing mesquite. "Bet you're glad you came, eh?"

"I . . . I . . . Vinny, this is—Can I call you Vinny?"

"You need a pill?"

"No, it's just . . . This is the best day of my entire life. I mean outside of marriage and births." Jim snapped his fingers. "I know what I'm going to do. I'll enlarge one of the photos and mail it to him as a present. I'll have it professionally matted, with a big, expensive frame. Think I got a good one of him and Mandy—"

"Jim, you have to be cool. If you're going to hang out, you can't act like some fruitcake fan. How do you want your steak?"

"Medium. That's the thing. He's got a million insane fans all over the country. . . ." Jim popped the exposed film canister out of the camera and stuck it in his pocket. ". . . He'll never remember me."

"Of course he'll remember you."

Jim shook his head. "But he might if he likes the photo. Then if I ever get to come back over, it would be neat if he recognized me."

Vinny hung steak tongs on the side of the grill, turned and squatted in a boxer's crouch. He playfully punched Jim in the stomach. "You're a crazy fuck, you know that? Wouldn't last five seconds in Jersey, but that's why I like you."

"Vinny . . ."

"No, really. You're one of the genuine good guys."

"Vinny . . ."

"It's so refreshing. I don't know any good guys, except Good Guy Moe. Saw him once take this meat hook—"

"Vinny . . ."

"What?"

"Fire."

Vinny turned. "Shit." He hit the grill with a glass of Bacardi 151. Bigger flames.

"Mandy, would you be a dear and grab some more steaks from the fridge."

"Sure, Vin."

She hopped up pertly and scampered inside. Seconds later Mandy slowly walked backward out of the house like she was at gunpoint. Her voice cracked as she called to the player: "Baby?"

"What is it?"

"Someone's here to see you."

The guys turned.

"What have you done with my husband!"

"Martha," said Jim. "What are you doing here?"

She marched around the pool and gave Vinny the toxic eye. He stared down at shoes he couldn't see. Then she stomped right up to——. "I don't care how famous you are! Stay away from Jim with your drugs and bimbos and mob buddies!"

The player shrank back on his lounger. ". . . Sorry."

Martha yanked her husband by the arm. "Let's go!"

The other two guys leaned and watched until they were sure she was gone, then the player looked at Vinny. "What the fuck was that about?"

"He's happily married."

TWENTY-EIGHT

GULF OF MEXICO

*T*he G-Unit arrived at the ballroom doors earlier than ever before, but the line was already around the corner.

"What's going on?" asked Edna.

"Those new dancers are what's going on."

This far back, it was over before it had begun. The doors finally opened, and the women resigned themselves to an evening of punch and cookies. They stared across the room at the flock of women swarming around the new guys.

"Why aren't they dancing?" asked Edna.

That's when she noticed Steve enthusiastically waving them over.

"What do you think he wants?"

Five minutes later, the G-Unit and the rest of the room couldn't believe the reversal of fortune: These new guys had fought off all comers, waiting for Edith and her friends, whom they now spun and waltzed around the floor.

Edith was beside herself. "Steve, you're a marvelous dancer!"

"Just following your lead."

"And such a gentleman . . . But why'd you wait for us?"

A charming smile. "You and your friends are special."

Edith's own blushing smile: "Oh, please . . ."

It went like that all night, every night, from Tampa to Cozumel and back again. The other women finally gave up, and the Brimleys were back in play.

CIA HEADQUARTERS, LANGLEY, VIRGINIA

Two agents returned to a dim room. One sat down at a computer; the other watched over her shoulder.

"Where's the ship now?"

"On its way back to Tampa," said Special Agent Denise Wicks.

"Any more on that chatter we picked up?"

"Nope. Just the name of the ship."

"Not even a time range?"

"We don't even know if they're planning anything."

"Agent Foxtrot now lives in Tampa. When they hit port, it would be easy to activate—"

"Still too risky."

"When did you first meet Foxtrot?"

"I don't know," said Wicks. "Sixteen, seventeen years ago? . . ."

KUWAIT CITY, 1991

Operation Desert Shield was still a week away. Iraqi soldiers roamed streets at will, tanks at both ends of a wide thoroughfare through the center of the previously thriving financial district. Now, broken glass and charred BMWs, every building pocked with machine-gun fire.

The street was normally jammed, but no traffic or pedestrians these days. The few Kuwaitis who hadn't been able to flee now hid in whatever cubbyholes the soldiers hadn't been able to detect when they'd swept the city. Troops milled in front of sacked storefronts. An Iraqi colonel walked down the middle of the road with his enlisted assistant. He had a thick, jet-black mustache, and he was laughing.

The assistant listened attentively as they continued up the street. The colonel stopped mid-sentence. The assistant looked sideways, then down. The officer lay in a spreading purple-red puddle from a silent forehead bullet. The assistant stood bolt straight, threw his hands up in surrender and didn't move. Nearby soldiers ran in directionless confusion; others rushed up the stairs of the biggest building at the end of the street, the one with the giant, ornate tower. Obvious sniper nest. That's why the shooter was down on street level, technically a few inches below, camouflaged in a dirt depression dug twelve hours earlier under cover of night.

By the time they reached the top of the spire, the sniper was gone like a ghost. The colonel's assistant remained motionless in the middle of the street, arms still up, and didn't move for the next three hours until sunset.

It went like that each day, all over the city, without pattern or clue. Psychological warfare. Top-ranking officers picked off by an invisible enemy. Five more colonels and a general. Regular soldiers left untouched, except cramped muscles from standing till dark.

The agent was the stuff of mythology, a proverbial lone wolf who could survive and inflict havoc for weeks behind enemy lines with no trace of ever having been there. It was years of training, but it was more. Logic dictated some fierce, bulging warrior appearance, but if you ran into the agent in a supermarket back home . . . well, the last person you'd expect. Because the most invaluable trait was that one-in-a-million mental makeup you can't teach. Even at the moment of the killshot, the agent's pulse never budged.

Code name: Foxtrot.

Desert Shield was launched. Kuwait liberated. They called Foxtrot in for new orders. The "Shield" became "Storm." The invasion of Iraq. First business: Control the skies. Ill-trained Iraqi pilots were no issue. The real danger came from anti-aircraft ground radar directing surface-to-air missiles. Stationary sites were bombed to molecules. The problem was a handful of mobile radar trucks. By the time allied planes could trace the active ping, off they'd zipped.

Intelligence arrived. General headquarters location of a mobile squadron west of Mosul, trucks darting around at night, then returning to the concealment of a building or overhead netting, where they were protected by platoons of elite commandos.

Foxtrot's mission: forward recon thirty miles beyond the nearest other American. Locate the radar trucks using any technique available, then break radio silence with the air-base. When the F-16s were in range, Foxtrot would laser-paint the target. Only one problem. Once radio silence was broken, Foxtrot would also be a target. The plan had no escape clause.

The first moonless night, a two-seat special-ops dune buggy dropped the agent in a sea of sand. It took most of the evening for Foxtrot to avoid Iraqi patrols and cover the remaining ground on foot until the first lights of Mosul danced along the flat horizon. Then two more hours flanking quickly in the cool night desert, following the sounds of the returning radar trucks and confirming the base with a night-vision scope.

Time got tight. A hole was quickly dug as the sky began to lighten. Camouflaged cover fashioned. Foxtrot burrowed in with the radio and laser. The plan was rolling smoothly.

Then the wheels came off.

TWENTY-NINE

FOXTROT

angley, Virginia: one year after the mission in Iraq.

Brown, leafless trees. Scattered crusts of snow dotted the shoulders of the parkway as spring began its thaw. A sign at the heavily guarded entrance: CENTRAL INTELLIGENCE AGENCY.

The low building sprawled. Somewhere deep inside, another black-box debriefing. This one had the tone of unofficial reprimand that would never see ink. Foxtrot sat respectfully and listened to the long table of superiors.

"You violated protocol."

"The mission was in your hands."

"You've never hesitated before."

"Why didn't you shoot the civilian?"

The questions weren't intended to be answered. Foxtrot's pulse was like a day at the beach.

"The directive is more than clear."

The purpose of the directive was to eliminate tough calls by making them ahead of time. The tougher the call, the greater the need for an advance decision. Then, all that remained was reflex.

This was one of the toughest calls of all, but that's why

they call it war. Foxtrot was too good to be detected in desert surveillance, except by accident: Always a slim chance that some peasant or farmer with world-class bad luck might stumble upon the one-person bunker and become curious about its camouflaged cover. The directive: If he lifts the cover, shoot him with a silencer-equipped sidearm, and pull the body inside with you. They'd gone over it dozens of times.

"What the hell happened?"

They expected an answer this time.

"Everything was going by the book," said Foxtrot. "Then the sun rose . . ."

. . . The sun rose out of the eastern sand with wavering lines. *Lawrence of Arabia*. The Anvil. Foxtrot switched to regular binoculars. Substantial Republican Guard presence but none the wiser. American planes already in the air. Just waiting for the word. A laser dot hit the side of a building; a hand reached for the radio.

A nearby sound. Right flank, five o'clock. Foxtrot turned toward a slit in the camouflaged lid. Vision was obscured, but one thing was certain: not military. Dammit. Foxtrot switched off the laser and slowly rolled over, bracing the pistol for a mandatory head shot if the unfortunate civilian raised the cover. Perfectly still. Seemed like forever. Sandy footsteps. *No, please, don't . . .*

Dusty hands raised the camouflage. Foxtrot's pistol aimed right between the eyes. For the first time ever, a skipped heartbeat. The trigger finger wouldn't respond. The civilian ran off sounding the alarm.

"Son of a bitch!" Foxtrot leaped from the hole and looped an arm through the laser backpack, then raced straight for the radar compound, radio mike in hand: " . . . *Bravo, Foxtrot. Deliver package . . .* " The radio was flung aside. The screaming civilian had troops scrambling out of buildings. Foxtrot ran straight for them. One of the Iraqis saw the apparition sprinting out of the desert. He began shooting, and the others joined in.

Bullets raked the ground at Foxtrot's feet. In the distance, an approaching roar of F-16 Falcons, pilots on the radio. "Where's that laser?"

The radar compound deployed two jeeps with .50-caliber mounts. The desert became alive with bursts of sand exploding all around Foxtrot, who never broke stride toward the trucks. Straight at death.

The direction and sound of the jets said they were five or six seconds out. Foxtrot dove belly down onto the sand and aimed the laser. The .50-calibers had been erratic from bounding over the dunes, but now the jeeps hit a flat stretch, and one of the gunners drew a bead. The strafing started sixty yards ahead and ripped through the sand on a direct line that would cut Foxtrot in half headfirst. The bullets reached fifty yards, forty, thirty—Foxtrot's right eye stayed glued to the laser sight—twenty, ten . . . the first guided bunker bomb hit. The concussion blew the gunners into the air and upended both the jeeps. Debris rained.

Back at the base, a bird colonel inspected videos from the F-16s' onboard cameras. Total success. But where was Foxtrot?

"Presumed killed in action," said the classified report.

Three days later, a security detail of U.S. soldiers chatted at a checkpoint on the Kuwaiti border.

Someone suddenly appeared right beside them.

"Shit!" They fumbled for M-16s before recognizing U.S. gear under all the filth. "Where the hell did you come from?"

"Can't tell you that," said Foxtrot.

LANGLEY, VIRGINIA

The story ended. People at the table shook their heads.

"Jesus," said Special Agent Denise Wicks. "I don't know

if I'm more pissed off by your insubordination or because the mission succeeded despite it."

Foxtrot didn't speak.

"Stand."

The agent did.

Wicks walked over. "I can't believe I'm doing this." She pinned a medal for valor on Foxtrot. "Congratulations."

"Thank you."

Then she unpinned it and put it back in her pocket, because the mission never existed.

They sat back down. Officialness over. Time for smiles.

"So, you're really leaving the service?" said Wicks.

"Doing the same thing too long. Thought I'd try something else."

"Like what?"

"Don't know yet," said Foxtrot, thinking back to the unforgettable face of that civilian in the desert who'd stumbled upon the camouflaged nest. A five-year-old girl.

"Where do you think you'll go?"

"Guess back home to Tampa."

THIRTY

TAMPA

*T*he sun waned on the grimy part of town past the old railroad depot. Two dozen men fidgeted in an alley of broken glass and blowing newspapers.

Serge had called another wildcat team meeting of Non-Confrontationalists Anonymous. He had his new video camera, and he was pumped!

If only they could get started. Serge had never met people with so many questions. Why did they have to wear costumes? And makeup?

"Because they'll give you the anonymity to role-play like you couldn't otherwise. Plus the comic relief of the outfits I picked—Well, if my hunch is right, I may just strike a previously undiscovered chord with the rest of the country, make a killing on the Internet and leave my legacy."

"Where's the moderator?"

"He'll be here any minute," said Serge. "Please, take your places. . . . Coleman, you ready with the camcorder?"

"Ready!"

Serge took a seat in a director's chair, raising a home-made cardboard megaphone. "And . . . *action!*"

Two of the group's members squared off like a pair of

kids on the playground who've never fought before. Lots of dancing around, then the occasional, awkward punch that only swishes air.

"Come on!" Serge yelled into the cardboard tube. "Fight!"

Five more minutes of passive jockeying until one of the timid swings accidentally found a cheekbone.

"Ow! Bastard! You hit me!"

"I didn't mean to! Are you okay?"

Wham.

"You hit me back! You fuck!"

"Sorry, don't know what got into me."

Wham.

"Perfect!" shouted Serge. "You're getting the hang of it." He turned to the rest of the group waiting against a brick wall plastered with rave-club flyers. "Okay, everyone else in!"

"But . . ."

"Get over there!"

They reluctantly joined the first pair. Another slow start. But the alley's close quarters precipitated more accidental punches, leading to deliberate ones. It grew nasty, the way only amateur hour can. Kicking, biting, hair-pulling. Then they went off Serge's script, picking up garbage cans, pipes and bottles.

"Coleman! This is incredible! You getting it?"

"Every second."

An Escalade drove up.

"Jim," said Serge. "You're late."

"They're killing each other! What the heck's going on?"

"I'm curing them."

"Serge!"

"There's still time for you to get in there—"

"We have to talk." Jim stepped aside. Someone flew by into a pile of boxes. "I can't take this anymore."

"Take what?"

"I saw on TV about that business at the railroad tracks. Why did you do that?"

"Me?"

"You're saying you didn't do it?"

"Jim, Jim, Jim, you must have more trust." He reached in his pocket. "Here."

"What's this?"

"Free tickets."

"Serge! Enough's enough!"

"I know you're upset right now. But think of Martha. Those tickets were expensive. You'll have a great evening."

Jim pushed them back. "If you want to do a favor, just leave us alone."

"But those tickets are guaranteed to help with your bedroom problems."

"I—You can tell?" A bottle smashed against the brick wall next to his head. "How'd you know?"

"Just use the tickets."

Jim took them and began reading. "What's this special service about?"

"I can't spell *everything* out for you. . . ." Serge raised the megaphone. "Phil! No cement blocks!"

GULF OF MEXICO

The G-Unit used to stay on board when the ship reached port. Didn't need the hassle of those insane Cozumel crowds. But then something changed, thanks to Steve and his foot-loose friends. A reawakened zest for life. They bought stylish sunglasses, purses and bright floral dresses from the ship's galleria. Laughter filled their stateroom. Hurricane glasses clinked, quarters tumbled into slot machines. Edna became a regular at the waterslide.

Then the ship hit port, and the G-Unit was first in line, casing security procedures.

"I see a crack," said Edna. "Everything goes through the X-ray for safety, but they only spot-check at the declarations table."

"We'll exploit it with our age."

They raced slow-motion down the gangway, hitting Mexico like spring-breakers. Bustling outdoor markets, cafés, snorkeling lessons, nightclubs. Then they returned to the ship and smuggled duty-free Kahlúa past security without question.

The gals locked the door to their cabin, and the room filled with giddiness.

Knock-knock-knock.

"Hide the liquor!"

Another knock.

". . . Just a minute." Edith eventually opened the door a slit. "What do you want?"

A steward smiled and cradled a bottle in a towel.

"What's that?"

"Champagne."

"We didn't order any."

"It came with a card," said the steward.

Edith grabbed the bottle and envelope.

The steward smiled with tip-ready hand. The door closed.

"What is it?" asked Eunice.

"I don't know." She set the bottle on a table and tore at the envelope.

"What's it say?"

"Will you wait?" Edith opened the card: FROM YOUR SECRET ADMIRERS.

"Who do you think?"

"I have a strong suspicion." Edith twisted the wire harness off the cap, stuck the bottle between her legs and grunted.

Pop.

"Ow!"

"Put ice on it."

TAMPA

The headless body at the railroad tracks wouldn't go away, thanks to the press.

Politics rolled downhill from the mayor to the police chief to the unfortunate agents in charge of the case. That would be Sadler and Mayfield. Both excellent homicide veterans, both overweight. In their spare time, Sadler liked to build scale model planes from scratch, and Mayfield didn't. It never came up.

The detectives had started the investigation with two desks, a shared phone and the distracting noise of a busy police office.

"What kind of a sick place are we living?" said Sadler. "This mess with the train, plus those nine deaths the FBI still hasn't solved."

"We're not supposed to talk about that," said Mayfield. "The press can't find out."

"They've already reported it."

"They reported the individual deaths. But they're just not supposed to know they're connected."

"Think *this* is connected?"

"Who knows?"

The TV affiliates wouldn't connect the nine deaths for some time, if ever, because it involved reading documents. The decapitation, on the other hand, was made to order for sweeps week. The mayor felt the heat, and otherwise austere resources flowed.

A task force was tasked. Fifteen top investigators reported to Sadler and Mayfield. They got a conference room and a water cooler. Phone company people installed new lines. Handcarts arrived with stacks of cardboard boxes: the victim's court records and his mobile home contents. Agents began unloading. Others cleared bulletin boards of thumb-tacked suspect photos from the last task force. A rookie dumped a handful of RICO mug shots in the trash.

Sadler walked seriously toward the front of the room. "Listen up everyone. We got a nightmare and no leads. Just a partial fingerprint from a pillow in the victim's mobile home. The lab guys are working on it. Meanwhile, we're starting from the beginning." He waved a thick stack of pages. "This is Bodine Biffle's record. We're going to track every codefendant, known associate, girlfriend, relatives, neighbor, and anyone who worked with him at Moving Dudes. I want to know if his dry cleaner had a parking ticket. . . ."

The room grumbled.

"Quiet down," said Mayfield. "If the answer's here, we're going to find it."

Into the afternoon: tedium, coffee, sandwiches, guys standing to stretch. Bulletin boards filled with fresh index cards. Investigators opened more boxes; others called out hundreds of potential cross-references to the rest of the room. No matches.

One agent peeled through recent receipts. ". . . Luck Pawn, Payday Check Advance, Caribbean Crown Line, Hubcap Emporium—"

"Back up," called an agent on the other side of the room. "Did you say, 'Caribbean Crown'?"

"Right."

"What is it?" asked Sadler.

"Sir," said the second agent. "We had someone go missing a few weeks back on a cruise out of here."

"Thousands sail from Tampa every week," said Sadler.

"This one had a rap sheet," said the agent. "And his body parts washed up in the mangroves at Terra Ceia."

"What ship?"

"Serendipity."

The other agent looked up from his cruise receipt. *"Serendipity."*

An hour later, everyone at the bulletin boards. The life history of the missing cruise passenger took shape: crime jacket, phone records, stolen Diner's Club—each shard of his existence assigned to a separate index card.

Someone pulled a card off the board. "Think we might have something. The motel where he stayed before boarding the cruise." The agent called a name across the room.

Another agent at another bulletin board: "It's a match."

"Excellent work," said Sadler. "Still a long shot. Travel agencies often bundle the same motels with the same ships. But worth checking."

Mayfield came up and grabbed one of the index cards. "More than worth checking."

"Why do you say that?" asked Sadler.

"I know this place. It's a shit hole."

"So?"

"You won't believe who owns it."

"Who?"

Mayfield had just told him when a breathless detective with a computer printout ran into the room. "Sir, database got a hit on that partial fingerprint."

THIRTY-ONE

DAVENPORT RESIDENCE

*J*im buttoned a freshly pressed shirt. "Martha? You almost ready?"

"Give me a minute. . . ."

"The reservations are for six."

The bathroom: "You've told me eight times."

"But for this we can't be a minute late. You know how long you always take to get ready—"

The door opened. "How do I look?"

Her racy new scarlet evening dress hit Jim in the stomach. Especially the strapless part.

Martha began to frown. "What's the matter?"

"Wow."

Her smile rebounded. "Was afraid you wouldn't like it."

"You kidding?"

She leaned over the dresser. "Just let me make sure I have all my stuff." Such a dress normally would have been accessorized with an elegant clutch purse. Instead, Martha rummaged through an oversized canvas Siesta Key beach bag, then hoisted it over her shoulder. "Think I got everything."

The Davenports headed out of the house. Jim held the passenger door.

"You're such a gentleman."

They drove a short five minutes to the south end of Davis Islands. The islands had a tail: this long, thick sand spit that curled in a crescent around a broad lagoon. A road ran atop the spit and ended at the exclusive Davis Islands Yacht Club. Along the way, the shore formed one of the hundred-odd Florida bathing areas nicknamed Beer Can Beach, where off-islanders created an economic pressure drop at the yacht club's gates. The lagoon inside the crescent was a squatters' community of houseboats and live-aboard schooners anchored in what was originally a 1920s seaplane basin. But the seaplanes were long gone. Today, wealthy locals landed their Cessnas and Piper Cubs just over the seawall on modest runways of the adjacent Peter O. Knight Airport.

Jim pulled into a parking slot at the airport's cozy terminal with retro parasol overhangs. "This is so exciting," said Martha. "I can't believe you actually planned this."

"Plus it's free."

"You remember the tickets?"

Jim flapped his hand. "Right here."

They went inside and took seats in a space the size of a doctor's waiting room. Martha practically bounced with anticipation. "I didn't even realize a service like this existed."

"Neither did I, but my friend knew all about it."

"The one from your support group who gave you the tickets?"

A booming horn blasted.

"What the heck was that?" said Martha.

Jim pointed out the window behind them. "Cruise ship."

Martha stared up at four tiny old ladies waving at the world from one of the towering top decks. "Holy cow! Looks like it's going to crash into the island!"

"There's a deep ship channel that runs along the east seawall," said Jim

"But it's so close."

"It's a narrow channel."

Martha stood and followed the ship around to the other windows. She watched it grow small in the bay. She looked at the western sky and watched something else grow large.

A blue-and-white twin-engine Beechcraft made its final approach, coming in low across the water. It cleared the fence at the end of the runway for an expert three-point landing.

"Is that ours?" asked Martha.

"I think so."

The eight-seater taxied past a row of private planes tethered to the side of the runway. The propellers spun to a stop. A glowing couple exited the plane, squeezing each other's arms and laughing. Then the pilot. He opened the terminal's back door and stuck his head inside. Red, sound-suppressing headphones hung around his neck. "Davenports?"

"Over here," said Jim.

"This way."

The trio walked across the tarmac.

"I've never done anything like this before," said Martha.

"Most people haven't," said the pilot. "Just relax and have fun. . . . Watch your step."

Martha climbed aboard. Jim was right behind with the tickets: TAMPA BAY MILE-HIGH CLUB.

The interior reminded Martha of a John Denver song. Shag carpet, dim lights, love bed. She pointed back at the midsection. "What's that?"

"Privacy partition," said the pilot, standing on the runway at the passenger hatch. "Just like the one I have behind my seat."

"Another couple's back there?"

"They were on the last flight and wanted to go around again."

"But—"

"Don't worry," said the pilot. "The engines are so loud it'll be like you're all alone." He closed the hatch.

"Jim," whispered Martha. "There's another couple."

"I'm sure they have better things than to worry about us."

"I don't know if I can go through with this now."

"Martha," said Jim. "I was happy the way things were. *You're* the one who wanted to spice things up with weird stuff."

"Not weird. Variety. There's a difference."

"You got variety here."

"On the other hand, it might help."

"What might?"

"Article in this women's magazine. Some people get turned on by having others in earshot. The whole risk of discovery. I could be one of those people."

"Could be?"

"I don't know. I've never tried. We've never tried *anything.*"

"Thanks."

"You know what I mean."

The pilot started the engines. Left prop jerked first and began spinning, then the right, faster and faster. He turned around in his seat and shouted over the growing noise. "Before I close the partition, I need to mention a few things. . . ."

"You have to give a safety talk on a flight like this?" asked Martha.

The pilot shook his head. "Been hassled by the police. They say I fall under the new adult-use ordinance. So when we reach international waters I'll ring this." He held up a small brass bell. "I'm supposed to tell you no fooling around until then, but that's your business. Also, when we hit 5,280 feet . . ."

"That's a mile," Jim whispered.

"I'm not an idiot," said Martha.

". . . I'll ring the bell again."

"Why?"

"Customers have asked."

"One question," said Jim. "How'd you get into this business?"

"Back in the day, people joined the mile-high club with quickies in lavatories of major airlines. Usually half-empty red-eyes from the Coast. But heightened security after nine-eleven created all kinds of new jobs like this." He closed the partition.

The Beechcraft raced down the runway. The sun had just set. A red beacon flashed on the plane's roof as wheels lifted off.

Martha reached in her tote bag and pulled out a giant, gleaming, state-of-the-art vibrator.

"Martha!"

"I know it's embarrassing. But it's *all* embarrassing to me. The magazines said I have to work through it if I'm ever going to discover my needs."

"You need that?"

"We'll find out. The articles said these things make some women have orgasms like earthquakes."

"I just can't picture you going up to a register and buying that thing."

"I wore sunglasses. And a hat and big coat."

"No mustache?"

"All the women were dressed like me."

"An adult store full of women?"

"It was the Todd, up at Fletcher and Nebraska. They market to women."

"How?"

"Cute curtains." She loaded four D batteries and screwed the back shut. Then she pulled a polishing rag from her bag and began buffing the sleek rocket.

"That thing looks expensive," said Jim.

"Most expensive they had," said Martha, rubbing extra hard on a particular spot. "If anything's going in me, it's got to be classy." She finishing buffing and hit a button. It roared to life like a leaf blower.

"Holy cripes," said Jim. "Did they have anything with more horsepower?"

"No."

"Martha, I want you to be happy, but—"

A bell rang.

"Here . . ." She handed it over and hiked up her dress.

"What do I do?"

"Surprise me." Martha lay back on the love bed and closed her eyes. "Just don't drop it."

Crash. The sound of batteries rolling across the cabin floor.

Martha opened her eyes. "Please tell me you didn't break it."

"No, the cap just popped off." Jim reloaded the batteries and screwed the end shut again. He hit the switch. Quiet. "Martha?"

"What?"

"It's broken."

"I can't have anything nice."

"Honey, this is our special night. Let's enjoy it."

The Davenports sat on the bed and held hands as they looked out the window at the darkening Gulf of Mexico. They exchanged mischievous looks and began giggling.

The bell rang again.

Martha pushed Jim down onto the sheets. She knelt and pulled the dress off over her head, revealing recent purchases from Victoria's Secret. Lace panties and pushups, both black.

"Good God!—"

She grabbed Jim's shirt collar with both hands. Buttons flew.

"Martha! What's gotten into you?"

"I don't know. This plane thing's a super turn-on. That's

why we have to try new stuff." She opened his belt but hit a snag. "What the fuck's wrong with your zipper?"

"Martha! Your mouth!"

"Goddamn this thing!"

"Let me get it. You'll rip skin."

"Just hurry!"

Jim pulled his pants down. "There."

Bam. She shoved him back down, climbed aboard and rode like a rodeo star.

"Who *are* you?" panted Jim.

"I don't know," said Martha. "But whatever you do, don't stop!"

BACK ON SHORE

A convoy of white government sedans raced north at the edge of the Gulf. All along the shore: towering new luxury condos that obliterated the strip's personality and stacked assholes thirty stories high.

The old roadside funk was gone: breakfast diners, beach bars, neon. All, that is, except for a few defiant hangers-on. One joint postponing a date with the wrecking ball was the kind of run-down, off-brand motel seen along the side of the highway with a swimming pool full of brown leaves and a single car in front of room 17 that makes passing motorists wonder, What's *his* problem?

A dozen sets of blackwall tires made the same screeching left turn and sped up the driveway under a crackling, half-burned-out sign:

HAMMERHEAD RANCH.

The people in the motel office heard squealing brakes.

Rafael Diaz looked out the window. "It's a raid! Run!" He and Benito hid in a closet.

Tommy Diaz casually arose from behind the registration desk. "Calm down. You look guilty." He walked to the office door, opened it with a jingle of bells and got a badge in the face.

"Detective Mayfield. This is Detective Sadler."

"To what do I owe the pleasure?"

"The two guys you murdered on my watch," said Sadler.

"Murders?" said Tommy. "That's terrible!"

"Cut the bullshit."

"Why? Am I a suspect?" said Tommy. "Do I need to call my attorney?"

"You're not charged with anything," said Mayfield. "Yet."

"We're legitimate businessmen. Why do you think we had anything to do with these tragedies?"

"Because both victims stayed here before taking cruises," said Sadler.

"And we matched your fingerprint to a pillow in one of the victim's homes," said Mayfield. "How do you explain that?"

"You just said he stayed here."

"So?"

"Must have stolen the pillow from his room," said Tommy. "My fingerprints are all over my own motel. Is that now a crime?"

Sadler held up a signed court document. "Search warrant." In the background, a battering ram came out of a trunk.

Tommy opened a desk drawer and handed Mayfield a large metal ring of brass room keys. "Use these. Wouldn't want the department to have to pay for accidental damage."

Mayfield tossed the ring to someone behind him. Then he stepped forward with an accusing finger. "You're going down."

"Is that kind of talk really necessary?" said Tommy. "I'm a big supporter of law enforcement."

A closet door creaked open. Rafael and Benito peeked out, heads stacked vertically.

"You messed up this time," said Mayfield. "We know what you're into."

"Please, enlighten me."

"Cocaine got too risky and expensive. . . ."

"Cocaine? You mean like on the TV?"

". . . That's where Bodine Biffle and Dale Crisp came in," said Sadler.

"Who?"

"The guys you killed," said Mayfield. "And we know why."

Sadler slapped the warrant on the front desk. "They were smuggling antiquities for you."

"Antiques?" said Tommy.

"*Antiquities,*" said Sadler. "Pre-Colombian. From the Yucatán. Tulum, Chichén Itzá."

"Fascinating story," said Tommy. "Quite an imagination. Are you writing a book?"

"We refreshed ourselves with your criminal record. Big-time smugglers. Just changed rackets."

"Detectives . . ." Tommy shook his head with a dismissive smile. "Those other matters are part of the distant past. We're respectable innkeepers now."

"What happened?" asked Sadler. "Figured it would be more profitable to whack your mules instead of paying them?"

Tommy's smile was unflappable. A diamond glistened in a gold front tooth.

"Just before coming over here, we reinterviewed witnesses," said Mayfield.

"Educated Biffle's girlfriend about accessory after the fact . . ." said Sadler.

". . . And she spilled everything. The cruises, black-market artifact trade. Moving Dudes didn't pay too good, so he did a little moonlighting for you bringing statues in."

"What's that word they use in court?" Tommy tapped his chin. "Oh, yes. *Hearsay.*"

The two detectives began walking out. Sadler turned at the door. "Your days are numbered!"

Tommy laughed. "If I didn't know better, I'd say that sounds like police harassment."

"It is."

Tommy maintained the sparkling smile until they were out of sight, then dropped it. "Will you idiots get out here?"

His brothers crept from the closet. "Are they gone?"

"No, they're tossing the place."

"We're going to jail!" said Benito.

"They don't have squat or we'd already be wearing bracelets." Tommy grabbed a pointy paper cup from a wall dispenser and stuck it under a water tap. "You're reacting exactly how they want."

"What are we going to do?"

Tommy glanced toward a wall calendar from the Mexican Board of Tourism.

THIRTY-TWO

EXACTLY ONE MILE HIGH OVER
THE GULF OF MEXICO

*I*t was the best sex they could remember since the kids were old enough to talk.

"Oh, Martha!"

"Oh, Jim!"

"Let's buy a plane!"

"Okay!"

Other side of the privacy partition: *"Jim? Jim Davenport? Is that you?"* The partition unsnapped. Serge poked his head through, wearing a Batman mask. "Thought I recognized your voice."

"Jesus!" Martha covered her breasts and rolled off her husband.

Jim stared in speechless horror.

Serge stared back. "This a bad time?"

"Jim!" said Martha, grabbing the dress to cover herself further. "Who the hell is that?"

"Martha," Jim said in a trembling voice. "This is my friend from the support group who gave us the tickets. Remember how you said I couldn't reveal his name?"

Martha made an angry motion with her eyes for Jim to get rid of him.

"Listen," Jim told Serge. "Don't you think you need to get back to whoever you're with—"

"Her name's Rachael."

". . . back to Rachael."

"It's okay," said Serge. "I'm just getting a B.J. now. I can talk."

"What?"

"In fact, it makes me *want* to talk. Hard to believe, but Peter O. Knight used to be Tampa's main airport. I can see it all now, silver DC-3s, alligator suitcases. . . . Rachael, watch the teeth . . . the terminal decorated with the 1930s art deco murals of George Snow depicting the history of flight, Daedalus to the Wright Brothers and Tony Janus, restored and on display at Tampa International's Airside E, for those keeping score at home . . ."

"Jim!" yelled Martha.

"Where are my manners?" said Serge. "Rachael, get up here. There are some people I want you to meet."

Catwoman stuck her head through the partition. "Meowwwww!"

"What a coincidence!" said Serge. "Can't believe you used your tickets the same night! We'll have to go out like this more often."

Catwoman's tongue went in Serge's ear. "Well, that's the old Bat Signal. Later . . ." The partition closed.

Martha reclined on the bed and folded her arms rigidly.

Jim went to touch her. "Honey . . ." She flinched away.

Jim fell back and stared at the plane's ceiling. They lay in frosty silence.

Not totally silent. Despite the engines' drone, conversation began filtering through the partition.

". . . You remember the Davenports," said Serge. "I've mentioned them a dozen times."

"Oh, that's right," said Rachael. "The dorky couple."

"They are *not* dorky," said Serge. "Just haven't been around the block like you and me. That's why I got them the tickets."

"You wasted your money," said Rachael. "They wouldn't know what to do if they had diagrams."

"They're just having a difficult time sexually."

"He told you about it?"

"Every detail. His wife's trying to get him into all this kinky shit, but so far nobody's come."

Martha covered her face in mortification.

"Why do you have such lame friends?" said Rachael.

"They are not lame."

"Yes they are!"

"I'm warning you!"

"What are you going to do, hurt me?"

"You'll beg for mercy."

"You wouldn't dare!"

"Oh yeah? How about this. Does that hurt?"

"Oh, God it hurts! It hurts, you fucker!"

"And this?"

"That hurts, too! Stop! Please! Owww! . . ."

"And this!"

"That does it!" snarled Rachael. "Your cock's going to get it now!"

"Owww!" yelled Serge.

"And this!"

"Yowwwwwww!"

On the other side of the curtain: Jim felt his shoulder poked. He turned.

"Jim," said Martha. "You're absolutely not going to believe what I'm going to say next. *I* don't even believe it."

"What?"

She glanced toward the partition. "They're getting me incredibly aroused."

"You're right. I don't believe it."

She threw her dress aside and climbed on top of Jim. "Have you been listening to them?"

"Not trying to."

"Think you remember most of it?"

"Martha, what are you asking?"

She found the right position, slid down onto him and gritted her teeth. Her voice changed to something Jim hadn't heard before: "You wouldn't dare hurt me!"

"What?"

"You're hurting me! You're hurting me!"

"I'm not doing anything! I swear!"

"Your cock's going to get it now!"

"Martha, you're scaring me!"

On the other side of the partition:

"I'll fucking kill you!" shouted Rachael. "Take that, you no-good motherfucker!"

"Why you mangy cunt!" yelled Serge.

"Wait, stop."

"What's the matter?"

"Our sex life is in a rut," said Rachael. "Fantasy role-playing."

"What about it?" asked Serge.

"We should try it," said Rachael. "We're always just being ourselves."

"Who do you want to play?"

She glanced toward the partition.

"You're joking."

"Who can explain sex? Their clumsiness is making me hot."

Other side of the partition: Martha was bucking so wildly that Jim had to grab her hips to keep her from being thrown clear. Screaming her head off: "Oh yes! Oh yes! Oh yes!" Just about to explode, when . . .

"Martha," said Jim. "Why'd you stop?"

She looked toward the partition. "Listen . . ."

From the other side:

"Oh, Martha!"

"Oh, Jim!"

"I don't know how to fuck!"

"Me neither!"

"How do we do it?"

"Give me that tiny needle-dick of yours."

"Is this the right hole?"

"Oh, Martha!"

"Oh, Jim!"

Martha rolled onto her back again. "How can this possibly get any more embarrassing?"

The partition opened. Batman pointed at the floor next to their bed. "You using that?"

Silence.

"Thanks." Serge grabbed the broken vibrator.

The partition closed.

THIRTY-THREE

918 LOBSTER LANE

*F*irst thing the next morning, a rusty Comet pulled
up the driveway.

    The home's front door was already open. Gay-
lord Wainscotting wheeled a last piece of luggage down to
the curb, where Mrs. Wainscotting and ten other suitcases
were already assembled in descending order of height, including Mrs. Wainscotting.

A limo arrived. The driver loaded bags.

Gaylord shook Serge's hand. "Thanks for doing this."

"Enjoy Cape Cod."

"Enjoy the club."

The chauffeur placed the final item in the trunk and
slammed the hood. Wainscotting climbed into the backseat.
The window rolled down. "Treat the place like your own,
unwind a little."

"I'm slammed," said Serge. "Work . . ."

"You can work anytime. Have some fun."

Serge shook his head. "Way behind deadline. We'll be
quiet as mice. In fact the neighbors probably won't even know
anyone's home."

"Glad I hooked up with you," said Gaylord. "All kinds of

cautionary tales about hiring the wrong house-sitters. One guy from the club had his place burned to the ground."

"She couldn't be in better hands," said Serge.

"Just don't work too hard."

"No other way."

Gaylord laughed. The limo drove off.

Serge whistled a blissful tune and strolled toward the house. He opened the front door. Stereo blasting, Coleman filling shot glasses, Rachael . . . Where was Rachael? A drum-roll of shattering glass from the kitchen. *"Goddammit!"*

Coleman cradled a phone receiver against his shoulder and knocked back bourbon. *" . . . Sure you don't need directions? . . . Yeah, it's going kick out the motherfuckin' jams. Later . . . "* He hung up and dialed again. "Hey, Serge . . ."

"What are you doing?"

"Shots."

"No, the phone."

Coleman put up a finger for Serge to hold a sec. *"Thumper? Coleman . . . No, I don't have the money. Listen, what are you doing Saturday? . . . "*

Coleman hung up and dialed again.

"I'm waiting," said Serge.

"Calling people for my party . . ." Coleman placed his spherical black-and-white TV on the counter and slapped the side. *" . . . Psycho Sal? Coleman . . . You still have to wear the ankle monitor? . . . "*

"Party?"

"Going to be killer!"

"Have you lost your mind? We can't throw a party!"

Coleman hung up again. "Serge, it's the ultimate party pad." He slapped the TV.

"We've been entrusted with the care of this house," said Serge. "The guy's only been gone a minute, and you're already sowing the seeds of destruction."

"Relax. Just a few of my closest friends." He dialed the phone and slapped the TV. "Serge, you know how to fix this thing?"

"Just keep slapping."

Rachael came into the room with a giant sterling service tray. She set it on the dining table, dumped a generous pile of white powder and began cutting rails with a razor blade.

Serge stood in amazement. "And just what do you think you're doing?"

Rachael leaned with a straw. "What the fuck's it look like?"

"You're scratching their tray all to hell!"

"Eat me!" Diver down.

" . . . *Slasher? Coleman* . . . " Slap.

Rachael pinched her nose. "Coleman, crank the stereo!"

"It's already up the whole way."

" . . . *We won't get fooled again!* . . . "

Coleman was about to make another call when he saw what Rachael was doing and dashed over to the table. "Can I have some?"

She shielded the tray like a protective mama bear. "Mine!"

"But you got plenty."

"Get away!"

"Give me some!"

"Let go of me!"

"Just a little bump! . . . Ow! . . . Serge! She's going for my balls!"

"They're trained to do that. Directive Seven."

The wrestling match was inelegant and vicious. They rolled across the floor and slammed into a table leg. A silver tray crashed to the ground.

They stood and stared down in mute horror. Rachael punched Coleman in the stomach. "Now look what you did!"

"Shit. Okay, we can salvage this," said Coleman. "I've

been here before. Stay perfectly still. Don't create any air currents until the haze settles."

Serge witnessed unprecedented discipline from his stationary companions.

Finally: "Now!" said Coleman. They dropped to their knees, herding dust with their hands and licking.

Serge headed up the stairs. "I wash my hands of this fiasco."

The widow's walks of Tampa's waterfront mansions were perfect for telescopes and binoculars. People watching big ships or sunsets or stars at night.

Serge's binoculars were aimed in a different direction, down the street. Jim Davenport's head filled the twenty-magnification view field.

Coleman came up the stairs with a bottle of Rémy Martin by the neck. "What are you doing?"

Serge adjusted the focus as Jim walked across his lawn with a ladder. "Protecting our friend. So far, so good. No sign of McGraw."

Coleman looked toward Serge's feet. "What's the rifle for?"

"In case McGraw slips under my perimeter and I can't get down there fast enough."

Coleman turned toward the bay. "There's a bunch of people in kayaks and canoes behind that other house. . . ."

"Hold it! Trouble! Oh my God!"

"What is it?"

"Jim's replacing a floodlight, but he's a step too high on the ladder. The one with the yellow warning label of a stick figure falling off a ladder."

"Serge, who's that over there walking toward him?"

"Where? . . . Oh, no!" Serge grabbed the rifle and chambered a round. Crosshairs tracked a stranger heading toward the house. He began pulling the trigger. He stopped.

Coleman took a swig. "Why aren't you shooting?"

Serge set the rifle down. "Just the UPS guy." He picked up the binoculars. "Sure wish Jim would get off the top step. Doesn't he know that's insane?"

"The kayaks and canoes are now behind our house."

Serge swung the binoculars toward their backyard. "Rachael's just sunning herself naked." The binoculars panned back the other way. "Picked up a second bogie."

"Bogie?"

"Martha. Heading for their car . . . Jim's calling to her, but she's ignoring him. Now he's waving for her to stop backing out of the driveway and . . . He fell off the ladder! Jim's down! Jim's down! . . . He's up! Martha patches out! Jim's running down the street after her! She's gone."

"What was that about?"

"They had a monster fight. Poor Jim. I know I'm being tough on myself, but I can't help think I'm almost responsible."

"Why's that?"

"Martha was crying inconsolably when our plane landed last night, even though I fixed the vibrator for free. I chased her out the passenger hatch, waving it in the air to give it back, but she just wailed louder and nearly went into one of the propellers."

"That would have sucked."

"I need to make it up to Jim." Serge lowered the binoculars and started downstairs.

Jim Davenport had moved his ladder to the northeast corner of his home. Just a few more twists on the floodlight.

The bushes below: "Psssst! Jim! You're one step too high!—"

Jim looked down.

"It's me, Serge. . . ."

Thud.

"Jim!" Serge leaped from the shrubs and bent over his

him as just another obsessed fan. In Pittsburgh, however, regulars at one popular sports bar said not so fast on calling off the rush to judgment. From our sister station, News Action 4 . . ."

Screaming drunks in Steelers jackets and Afro wigs crammed their faces in the camera. " . . . *That [bleep]hole is [bleep]ing dead! . . . " "Yeah! [bleep]ing dead!" "He's [bleeped] . . . " "Steelers [bleeping] rule! . . . "*

The broadcast switched back to Tampa. "In other news, our Action 7 Investigative Eye on Florida Team has turned up additional developments on the controversial new series of Internet videos that make *Bum Fights* look like *Teletubbies*. As reported earlier, an anonymous individual has struck a chord across the entire nation, which experts attribute to a political backlash against the French. Meanwhile the tapes continued selling like wildfire on eBay before the popular auction site shut down all bidding just before noon. But not before our own Action 7 investigative reporter Bannister Truth was able to obtain a copy and track Web sales to a computer at the downtown Tampa library."

The TV switched to a newsman dramatically thrusting a video box toward the camera. CLOWNS VS. MIMES VOL. III, THIS TIME IT'S PERSONAL! "The tape is too disgusting to watch!" said the reporter. "Let's take a look. . . ."

The broadcast cut to a clown slamming a car door on a mime's head.

"Breaking news!" the anchorwoman interrupted. "Police are just now responding to the site of a grisly discovery in the bay . . ."—the screen showed a night view from the Channel 7 chopper—". . . where the disfigured body of a scuba diver was found banging against a seawall on Davis Islands . . ."

Serge finished watching the news from the couch in Gaylord Wainscotting's living room. The set clicked off. He walked to the back of the dark house and saw a helicopter spotlight sweep over the water.

Three houses up, a squad of detectives combed Jim Davenport's backyard.

"What kind of monster? . . ."

"I've never seen anything so horrible. . . ."

Police divers were in the water. They finished securing the corpse to a special litter. One gave the thumbs-up. Others began hoisting.

A uniformed officer approached the detectives in charge. "Just got an ID. McGraw, Lyle."

They watched the body come over the wall.

"Anyone who'd do such a thing is a complete psycho," said Sadler.

"I'm not even sure what I'm looking at," said Mayfield.

"A floater. They all bloat like that."

"Not like *that*," said the coroner, bending down for a closer look at the human puffer fish. "He hasn't been dead long enough for gases to build up from decomposition."

"Then what caused?—"

"I know what it looks like," said the coroner, "but there's no possible way."

Silence.

The coroner looked up. They were waiting.

"At least I *hope* it's not what I think." The coroner stood. "You heard rumors about terrorists planning to use scuba divers to attach magnetic bombs to the hulls of our ships?"

A few nods.

"Then you may also have heard those leaked reports about classified military programs training dolphins to patrol our ports, because their sonar is better than our most advanced hydrophones."

"But we don't have any dolphins around here like that," said Sadler. "Right?"

"That's where it gets tricky," said the coroner. "The Navy

denies it, but there's word of a special training facility in Key West."

"And?"

"They came up a couple dolphins short after Hurricane Wilma."

"Holy mother . . ."

"I don't understand," said Mayfield. "Even if a dolphin detects a scuba diver, how does it stop him, let alone cause this kind of mess?"

"The dolphins are fitted with a special weapon," said the coroner. "Believe me, it's one of the last ways you want to go."

"What kind of special weapon?"

EARLIER THAT NIGHT

"Serge," said Coleman, "my arms are getting tired."

"Just keep rowing."

"Why can't *you* row?"

Serge scanned the water off the starboard side with a night-vision monocular. "Because I'm on lookout—and I have to operate Serge's New Secret Weapon. It's a lot to deal with in a canoe."

Oars splashed in the moonlit bay. "I still don't understand how that thing works. All I know is you destroyed my laughing-gas dispenser."

"Your sacrifice for the community is duly noted."

"But it cost me ten bucks at a Bourbon Street head shop."

"It only made you fall down a lot."

"That's the whole point."

"Shhhhhhhhhhh!"

Coleman stopped rowing. "What is it?"

Serge peered over the side. "We have activity."

For the last hour, their canoe had slowly made its way

east from a boat launch across the harbor at Ballast Point, until they were now fifty yards off Davis Islands. In the green glow of Serge's nightscope, a figure in a black wet suit silently swam toward the seawall behind the Davenport residence.

The scope following a trail of bubbles. "Row to the right. . . . A little more . . . Okay, stop." Serge reached into the bottom of the canoe. "Almost over the diver. We'll drift the rest of the way with the tide."

"Can you see him?"

"Perfectly."

"What's he doing?"

"Stopping. He knows we're here."

"So your plan's ruined?"

"Naw, he just thinks it's a coincidence. Couple of health nuts out at night in a canoe. He's trying to remain undetected until we pass."

Serge grabbed his New Secret Weapon.

"What's he doing now?"

"Looking up at us. Good. Otherwise this thing might glance off the scuba tank. . . . Come on, just a little farther. . . . Almost over him . . . allllllllmost . . . Now!"

Serge quickly raised the harpoonlike device and thrust it down into the water with his right hand. His left grabbed a short, makeshift length of PVC pipe that rose three-quarters of the way up the spear's shaft, and gave it a fast twist.

Coleman cracked a Schlitz. "Where'd you get the idea for that thing?"

Serge maintained a firm two-handed grip as the pole jerked wildly. "Top-secret U.S. Navy program. Training dolphins in Key West to patrol ports for scuba-diving terrorists."

"But dolphins are so nice," said Coleman. "Would they actually attack a terrorist?"

"Not remotely," said Serge, still gripping the pole. "So they make a game of it by teaching dolphins to playfully tap their handlers in the chest with a small cylinder attached to their snouts." He jerked the weapon out of the water and laid it back in the bottom of the canoe. "The cylinders are empty during training. But during live patrol, they're loaded with a capsule of highly compressed gas and fitted with a spring-loaded needle. Very effective. And messy, one of the worst ways to go . . . ."

The bloated diver bobbed to the surface like a cork, quivering next to the canoe.

" . . . Chest cavity inflates with a massive amount of air, rupturing whatever internal organ took the needle and slowly crushing surrounding ones. . . . ."

"I think he's trying to yell."

"Going to be hard with collapsed lungs."

Coleman finished his beer and watched the diver twitch with after-tremors. "But how did you make one of those secret Navy weapons from my nitrous dispenser?"

"You know how you stick the whip-it canisters inside the dispenser and twist it to puncture the seal, filling those balloons you suck to get high?"

"In my sleep."

"I just substituted one of those carbon-dioxide canisters they use in paint-ball guns. Same size. And where the balloon usually goes, I welded a glue syringe from The Home Depot. Then I mounted the whole thing on the end of a broomstick, and slipped a length of PVC plumbing pipe over it so I could twist the puncture mechanism from a safe distance. . . . ."

The motionless diver began drifting away.

" . . . And from there, the science of hydraulics takes over. Wait, not exactly hydraulics because fluids don't compress like gas. Hey, I just flashed on another installment of Great Moments in Florida Hydraulics History."

"Go for it."

"Remember when Disney World first opened Hall of the Presidents?"

"The robots only went up to Nixon then."

"Good one, Coleman. Impressed you retained that."

"I was on acid, and Nixon's cheeks turned into a killer octopus."

"True fact: The hydraulic fluid they originally used in the robots was red. But soon after the curtains went up on the exhibit, they switched to clear."

"Why?"

"During one of the first shows, Abraham Lincoln is in the middle of his speech, and a hydraulic line busts. All this red stuff starts spraying like a Monty Python skit. Audience is horrified. They thought Disney was doing the assassination."

Coleman resumed paddling as the tide banged the diver against the seawall. "Why do you remember stuff like that?"

Serge grabbed his own pair of oars. "It keeps me happy."

THIRTY-FIVE

COZUMEL

*A*nother perfect day in paradise. Local merchants began to drool. Ten minutes earlier, an arriving cruise ship had a massive bowel movement of tourists, who would soon clog the streets with American currency.

The G-Unit was on a roll. The night before, Edna hit two hundred bucks on a slot, and Eunice scored another eighty at blackjack. Time to throw around a little of that cash. They shopped and ate and lounged at a sidewalk café that served margaritas in glasses the size of goldfish bowls. Then more kiosks and haggling into the siesta hours, until it was time to head back. Which meant the duty-free shop.

Edith hunched over a park bench, jamming vodka deep into a jumbo straw tourist purse with Mexican flags and sun gods.

From behind: "Edith!"

"I'm not doing anything!"

Steve and the other ballroom guys walked toward them with those toothy smiles. "Love the T-shirt."

Edith looked down at her oversized tie-dye: 51% ANGEL, 49% BITCH. DON'T PUSH IT. She looked up. "Thanks for the champagne."

"Me?" Steve said coyly.

"What are you doing here?" asked Edna.

"Same thing as you. Shopping. Find anything good yet?"

Edith opened her straw bag. "Just booze."

"Have to fix that," said Steve. "We can't allow you to leave without a real piece of the Yucatán. I know these great little out-of-the-way shops. . . ."

An hour later, the women lugged bulky bags crammed with native gifts. A chicken ran by. They entered a deserted store at the end of an alley.

One shopping bag was lighter than the rest.

"Why aren't you getting stuff?" asked Eunice.

Edith picked up a knight from a hand-carved Aztec chess set. "Haven't seen anything I like yet."

"So what? Those guys are paying."

A grinning salesman appeared from nowhere. "You like chess set? Special price. Fifty dollars."

She put the knight down. "I don't play chess."

"Special price for new players. Ten dollars."

"You just said fifty."

"Five dollars."

"I don't know. . . ." She picked up a piece of onyx.

The salesman smiled. "You like hash pipe? Twenty dollars."

Edith set it down.

". . . Three dollars . . ."

She nearly crashed into Steve on the way out of the shop.

He smiled again, arms behind his back. "Pick a hand."

"What?"

"Just pick."

"Okay, the left."

Steve produced a gift-wrapped box the size of a toaster.

"For me?"

"Saw you were having trouble deciding, so I got a surprise. Something I know you'll love."

Edith raised it to her right ear.

"No!" Steve's arms flew out. "Don't shake it!"

"Fragile?"

"Very."

The other women gathered around.

"This is so exciting. . . ."

"Wonder what it could be. . . ."

Edith grabbed the tail of a ribbon and began to pull.

"Don't open it here," said Steve. "Wait till you're back on the ship. You'll have a special treat to look forward to."

She held it toward him. "I can't accept this."

Steve sternly pushed it back. "You must."

"But you've already spent too much on us."

"My feelings will be hurt."

"Okay," Edith said reluctantly. "Thanks."

Steve waved and headed off with his pals. "See you tonight in the ballroom."

"Wouldn't miss it." Edna put the box to her ear and shook it.

They took an open-air shuttle to the dock and headed up the gangway. A cheery ship's officer swiped their magnetic ID cards through the reader. Green lights. The women hoisted gift bags onto the X-ray belt.

"Wasn't that nice of them?" said Edna.

"Such gentlemen," said Eunice.

They retrieved their belongings from the other side of the belt, and started for their cabin.

"Excuse me? Ma'am? . . ."

They kept walking.

"Ma'am, stop!"

"What's that shouting about?" Edith turned around.

"Ma'am, would you please come back here?"

"What for?"

"Spot check. Place your bags on the table."

"It's okay," said Edith. "You've never checked us before."

"We need to check this time."

"But I don't fit the profile."

"That's why we have to check you," said the officer. "So the people who fit the profile don't get sore."

She haltingly placed her bag on the table. Hands reached inside. Vodka came out. "Ma'am, you were supposed to declare this."

"I was? I mean, how'd that get there? I'm confused. Are you my son?"

"It's all right, ma'am." He placed the bottle on another table behind him. "We'll just hold it for you until we get back to Tampa." He reached in the bag again. A gift box came out. "What's this?"

Edith shrugged.

"I'll have to open it." The ribbon and wrapping paper came off. He lifted the lid and peeled back packing tissue, revealing a dusty, clay Mayan figure.

Edith put on her glasses. "What's that?"

"Just a Chac-Mool."

"A what?"

"Common souvenir." He returned it to the bag and handed it back. "I've gotten all my relatives one."

TAMPA

Serge sat in the front of the support-group meeting room. Two minutes till the next session. The place was full. Nobody had bothered to change since the latest video shoot.

The moderator entered from the back door. He took one

step and stopped at the sight. Dozens of bruised clowns and mimes, costumes torn, makeup caked with dried blood, one of them flicking a switchblade open and closed. The moderator began walking again, but much slower. He reached the podium with a blank look. "Serge, what's going on?"

"We can't tell you."

"What?"

"It's like *Fight Club.*"

"Fight Club?"

Ronald McDonald removed a toothpick. "The first rule of Clowns versus Mimes . . ."

The rest joined in: ". . . is you don't talk about Clowns versus Mimes."

The moderator stared helplessly at Serge. "I should have known you were behind this whole thing when I saw it on the news."

"Thank you."

"I wasn't saying that in a good way."

"Why not? I just gave America what it wanted before it knew it wanted it: clowns, mimes, bone-jarring violence, something for the entire family."

"But these people came here for help."

"And I cured them."

"Cured them? You've only made things worse! I'll have to double the meeting schedule just to repair your damage!"

"No offense," said Serge. "But they just dropped by out of politeness to say good-bye. They've outgrown your meetings."

"Wrong! They need to attend now more than ever!"

A white-faced man in a French cap placed two fingers on his forehead, like horns, then assumed a squatting position in the aisle next to his chair.

"What's that about?" asked the moderator.

A birthday-party clown held a magazine up sideways, letting the *Playboy* centerfold unfurl. "He says your meetings are bullshit."

"Please," begged the moderator. "Before it's too late. Stop listening to Serge!"

"Screw you!"

"Bite me!"

Mimes silently grabbed their crotches.

Ronald threw his toothpick aside and stood. "Fuck this lameness."

They got up and left en masse.

"Wait," said the moderator. "Come back! . . ."

SOUTHERN PENNSYLVANIA

Four A.M. Traffic was light as Interstate 79 wound through the hilly, dark countryside.

A Chevy van pulled away from a rest stop at the state line and headed south. The spare tire on the back had a Steelers wheel cover. The half dozen men inside discovered that their sixty-quart cooler was dangerously low on Miller.

All week long, TV reports from Tampa had been causing quite the stir inside a popular Pittsburgh sports bar. Then, on the seventh day of the news cycle, as the story began to fade and the clock edged toward closing time, people who had lives got back to them. Others ended up in the van.

One of the passengers talked into his cell and wrote something on the back of an envelope. "Thanks . . ." He hung up. "I got Davenport's address."

The driver looked over his shoulder. "Thought you said his phone was disconnected."

"Lucked out. I called this real estate friend of mine."

"At this hour?"

"I got him in trouble with his wife. There was screaming.